The Action at Redstone Creek

Center Point
Large Print

The Action at Redstone Creek

MERLE CONSTINER

CENTER POINT LARGE PRINT
THORNDIKE, MAINE

This Center Point Large Print edition
is published in the year 2025 by arrangement with
Golden West Inc.

The text of this Large Print edition is unabridged.
In other aspects, this book may vary
from the original edition.
Printed in the United States of America
on permanent paper sourced using
environmentally responsible foresting methods.
Set in 16-point Times New Roman type.

ISBN: 979-8-89164-427-4

The Library of Congress has cataloged this record
under Library of Congress Control Number: 2024947013

I

The man sat cross-legged on the dirt floor at the table, if you could call it a table, ax-cut to about four feet, and ax-split to a puncheon top, and looked at the coins before him: three silver quarters. His life savings, every cent in the world he could call his own. He wasn't too worried, because, somehow, he never could get the feel for money. But there were necessities, you couldn't get around that.

You couldn't make your own cartridges, for instance. He was completely unaware of this miserable shack he had recently built, and now lived in, back in a crotch of the Bitteroot Mountains, almost at their eastern base. He had lived half his life in the squalor of Apache villages down in Arizona where any food at all, say bitter wild cherries or wild potatoes or broiled burro was a ravishing delicacy.

His name was Mark Townsend. He was thirty-four, short, a little humped, big nosed, almost lizard eyed, and pretty ragged for the gaze of any white man. He had become a scout, guide, and interpreter for the cavalry out of San Carlos, had worked his way up to seventy-five dollars a month, and then got the overpowering notion to come up into this Idaho country and raise cattle.

His ability with weapons, in their simple killing qualities, was incredible, but his familiarity with gunfighters, outlaw or legal was hardly more than that of any other average westerner. He knew about death, though. He'd seen men killed like jackrabbits, and sometimes so terribly that few gunfighters could stand still and listen about it.

He had tried to start out by getting jobs at ranches, and had worked for a few, but couldn't hold a job. He didn't know too much about cows when you came right down to it, but that hadn't been his trouble. The trouble was that when he liked a man, he liked him, and when he didn't, he didn't, and sometimes didn't bother to handle that middle ground too much, not even as much as his Apache brothers. He'd been told he wasn't companionable, and worse.

It was midafternoon. He was staring at the quarters, trying to think of them in terms of cornmeal and fat pork, but thinking mainly what nice conchos they'd make, when the man stooped down and came in through the door.

"No offense meant," said the stranger, "but for a white man's shack, this place has a sort of stink, a little like Indian smell."

"Thank you," said Townsend. "Maybe some kindhearted Indian sometime will say as much for you."

Townsend appraised his unexpected visitor, and could come to no definite opinion on him, except he was a townsman, flashy, with two showy watchchains, and varnished boots. He was tall, gaunt, and sunken-eyed.

"Your name's Townsend. Right?" asked the man.

Townsend simply waited in silence.

"Mine's Joe Teague," said the man.

Townsend didn't even nod.

"I hear you're a pretty good tracker," said Teague.

"I've seen better," said Townsend, thinking of a couple of wizard trailers he'd known, old Chiricahuas. "But I stumbled around and made a living at it."

"I'm from over at Arnville," said Teague. Townsend had never heard of any Arnville. "I own the only saloon there, but I'm a poor man. You have to know that part when we start talking money."

If he thinks he's poor, thought Townsend, *he should have lived in some of the villages I've lived in!*

"I'm a poor man, but I'll give you a hundred dollars in gold to track and find a certain party for me," said Teague. He took five twenty-dollar gold pieces from a vest pocket, showed them, and put them back.

"No tracker," said Townsend, "would take on a proposition like that, depending on the finding part. Too many things can come between."

"Then I'll change it. I'll say if you do your best."

Townsend said, "That makes me like it even less. Looking at it from your point of view, you're taking too big a gamble. How do you know I won't take your money and scamper? And, all told, the price is mighty high."

"The price is high," said Teague, "because though I can tell you just about where the tracks start, nobody can't tell where they might go, how far. So you're taking a big gamble too."

"That's true," said Townsend. "Who is this party?"

"My son, so near and dear to me," said Teague urgently. "I scrimped and saved and sent him over the mountains to a college in Chicago, where he studied surveyin'. Well, sir, he got off the train at a place called Water Tank 43, in terrible rough country about twelve miles from here and started off to join a certain surveyin' party about forty miles away, dead into the mountains. They sent back a runner sayin' he got lost somewheres on the way. I want you to pick up his trail there by Water Tank 43—you can be sure there won't be many in that place—and find him for me. And bring new spirits to his old papa's heart."

"How old are they?" asked Townsend. "How long ago was this?"

"Not too long. I don't know exactly."

Thoughtfully, Townsend said, "I'll have to have a loaded packhorse. I've got a good tough mount, but I don't have supplies or a packhorse."

"They'll be there, waiting for you at the water tank. This'll be given to you by the man that gives you your money."

"What's this?" asked Townsend. "I don't get my money until I get there? I'll have to think this over."

"Oh, you'll get it all right," said Teague. "It'll be give to you by one of my closest friends. If you can't trust me, how can you expect me to trust you?"

After a moment's pause, Townsend said, "All right, I'll take it. How do I find this tank?"

"Jest go two mile east to the tracks. And follow them north to the tower."

There was no word of farewell as Teague left.

Townsend watched him go sardonically. This beloved son, so near and dear. Townsend was expected to find him but there had been no word of description of him, or of his horse, or even of his packhorse, if he had one. His name, his last name, must be Teague like his grieving papa's, but there had been no mention of any first name either.

This information, and probably a good deal more, he decided, he'd get from this friend who would be waiting for him at the tank to hand over the packhorse and the pay.

In the gray predawn of the morning next day, Townsend saddled his stumpy little tough muscled mare and started off. He didn't bother to lock his door, in fact he left it half open; most of his life he'd lived so there was little more to steal indoors than there was outside. He traveled light, hand-forged bowie knife which was as much a part of him as thumb and fingers, six-gun, which was so much a tool to him that he was scarcely conscious of it even when he was using it, and heavy, octagonal barreled rifle in its old castoff cavalry boot. Part of this thing, in fact, its main element, the touch that had provoked him and drawn him into it, was that old sensation he'd felt so many times before, on trail down in the mountains of Mexico, for instance, of trickery. He could resist women, under pressure he could resist liquor, but he couldn't resist trickery. So he had brought his own small reserve of food. A handful of jerky, in little rock-hard strips, in his side pocket.

According to his directions, he went two miles east, to the railroad tracks, and followed the rails north.

To his right lay the ever widening half cone of the valley, with its bottoms and fine grazing, and farther right but beyond sight, he knew, lay the great turbulent barrier of the Rockies. To his left, in the near distance, lay the scarcely less penetrable giant Bitteroots. The railroad edged the Bitteroots. This was country at the hem of spurs and foothills.

The terrible upthrusts behind them, now in full

leaf with their velvet coat of timber, showed their viciousness only now and then, in buff or cream patches of bare stone. Townsend took this stage of his journey easy, and arrived at the tank, set close to the track and ties, in the late afternoon. You couldn't miss the tank for there had been no other, and it had a big 43 painted on it.

Besides, there was a man and a packhorse in its shade, waiting.

The man was sitting on his haunches. He arose and mounted his saddlehorse as he saw Townsend approach. He was a tallish, skinny man, wearing two guns, each with its belt of cartridges, and, of all things, a bandolier of rifle cartridges crisscross from shoulder to opposite hip. He wore newish brown duck.

In spite of all this armament, and in spite of the newness of his clothes, Townsend got the feel from the way he sat his saddle that here was a man who had ridden much before.

And then, to his amazement, Townsend saw it was this Joe Teague himself. Part of it anyway made sense, Teague *would* be Teague's close friend.

Then, in sudden revulsion, an idea came to Townsend.

As he joined Teague, he said, "Where do you think *you're* going?"

"With *you,*" said Teague complacently.

"Oh, no you're not," said Townsend.

"Oh, yes I am," said Teague. "Or the deal's off."

And when you came right down to it, thought Townsend, why not? He had expected trickery and here it was.

"Why all the brass and cordite?" he asked curiously.

"I'm a great sportsman," said Teague, unsmiling.

"You'll slow me up," said Townsend, speaking honestly.

"I doubt it," said Teague. "In fact that will be one of my duties on the trail—what am I saying one of my duties, I mean my only duty—to see that you don't slow up."

A fury of blood surged to Townsend's temples.

Be companionable, he kept repeating to himself. Watch it. Be companionable.

He looked away a moment, looked back, and nodded, almost imperceptibly.

"Well, we've got to start sometime," said Townsend, "so we might as well start now." He began examining the earth. "Your son, I think you said son, was riding a sorrel and had a burro for a pack animal."

"Sorrel?" said Teague, scornfully. "The tracks tell you that, hey?"

"Tracks are only part of it," said Townsend. He pointed to a long horsehair caught in a splinter on the tank. "Mane-high," he explained.

Teague looked impressed.

Townsend said patiently, as patiently as he

could, "Here is your mount, and our packhorse. Here is my mount. This will be easy, if we can just keep finding them. Easy to remember. Burro and sorrel, they're both wearing these new kind of factory-finished shoes, the kind that come already made up for lazy blacksmiths, in number sizes."

They started off, Townsend and Teague, from the ends of the track ties, through an opening in the brush. In about a quarter mile, they came to a shallow creek. Townsend knew this must be the stream known as Redstone Creek. He said, "Here can be our first problem. If he went up or downstream it'll be hard but not impossible, by long odds. First we see if he went straight across."

They forded the stream and came out onto a cracked mud bank. "We're all right," said Townsend. "Here they are. We will keep going."

The country grew rougher, with rocky rubble, hard to trail and then impossible. "We just guess now," said Townsend. "And go straight ahead."

They were weaving their way along a sort of trail through great smooth boulders, some of them cabin-tall, when a voice behind them said steadily, "First, don't move. Now turn around, slow. Now up with those arms."

Two mounted men were behind them, one squinting over an aimed rifle, the other with his hands laxly on his saddlehorn. They looked like sorry chuckline cowboys, shabby, in everything but their well-kept weapons. They had the hard faces and dull eyes of killers.

The man with the aimed rifle said, “Howdy, Teague. All right, Bobbie, take up the collection.”

The man with his hands on his saddlehorn, dumpling faced, in his twenties, dismounted and took their weapons, Teague’s rifle and six-gun, Townsend’s rifle and six-gun. He grinned at Townsend’s heavy rifle. “Here’s an old-timer,” he said. “I wonder if it’ll reely shoot?”

The mounted man said, “Teague, who is your friend?”

“Him?” said Teague. “My camp servant. A livery stable helper I picked up. He’s not in this.”

The man with the rifle shot Teague from his saddle, then three times more as he lay on the ground, rapid fire, like drilling lead into a sack of seed corn.

They now turned their attention to Townsend.

“What do they call you?” asked the mounted man, lowering his rifle.

“Mac, mostly,” said Townsend innocently.

“Well, Mac, you’ll find your weapons uptrail a few hundred yards, on a rock,” said the leader. “This ain’t no country for a town bred livery stable feller to go around unarmed.”

Townsend, gnawed with curiosity, but on one point mainly at the moment, a professional point, asked, “How did you find your Mr. Teague?”

The mounted man said, “Bobbie’s a tracker.”

"Among my many other gifts," said the dumpling faced young man. "I'm a champion checker player, too."

"Where did you track him from?" asked Townsend.

The mounted man said, "He got off the Colorado train down the valley and took him a room in a hotel at a place called Sinton. Bobbie trailed him and his packhorse all the way from Sinton to here."

"Fo' and a half mile," said Bobbie.

"How does a fellow go about tracking?" asked Townsend.

"Well," said Bobbie. "A horse has four feet. When he walks or runs or anything them feet leaves little punch-holes in the ground. You follow them little punch-holes."

"But what if the ground is dry-packed, or it's rocky, or there's thick grass?"

"Then you hire a Cheyenne," said the mounted man. "I think he does it by sense o' smell."

"I ain't got time to answer no silly questions," said Bobbie.

"But you missed Mac, here, Bobbie," said the mounted man. "How come you happened to miss Mac?"

"Trackin' is a specialty, like checkers, say," said the fat faced young man. "You cain't do no day dreamin' at it. We was lookin' for Teague, wasn't we? And we found him, didn't we?"

Bobbie lapsed into silence, suddenly staring—at Townsend's feet.

"Say!" he exclaimed. "I never seen no moccasins like them afore! The toes turn up in front!"

Townsend, uneasily, being very careful to sound offhand, not especially interested, said, "I hear they're Apache style."

They had been made for him by his adopted grandmother. They were almost in pieces by now, but he loved them.

"Take 'em off!" ordered Bobbie.

Why die, thought Townsend? He removed them.

"I fancy 'em," said Bobbie, and stuffed them into the end of his bed roll.

The two men rode off, uptrail.

Townsend gazed at the dead Teague. He had noticed before that the varnished townsman's boots hadn't shown up today, and that Teague was wearing woodman's moccasins, but cobbler made, not Indian made. Teague was more tracking-wise than he showed. Townsend took off Teague's moccasins and put them on and walked around a little. They weren't too bad, a little stiff, a little large, but not too bad.

He turned Teague over and searched his pockets. Odds and ends but no money. Townsend found the money in a money belt, about two thousand dollars, in eagles and double eagles.

He took out a hundred dollars, the amount

agreed on, re-strapped the belt, tucked in Teague's shirt, pulled down his jacket. He rolled him back as he had been before, precisely and exactly as he had been before, and studied the surrounding terrain.

He then unbridled Teague's mount and turned the mare loose.

With the bit out of her mouth, she would easily survive.

He then took his packhorse's lead rope, mounted his own mare.

He continued uptrail.

His six-gun and rifle were on a slab of sandstone, waiting for him. Teague's were there, too. He left them untouched, taking his own.

He continued uptrail and kept his eyes glued on the ground. Soon he had added eight new hoofprints to his endless tracker's memory. These extra tracks soon vanished, expertly, and he was never again able to pick them up. But the new factory-finished shoes continued so he wasn't disturbed. They were somehow connected with the others, he was certain.

He was just fulfilling his contract made with Teague in his shack, he kept telling himself. Earning that hundred dollars.

He wasn't trying to get back his moccasins and a little vengeance, too, he kept telling himself.

And his face was hot because of the sun, not because he was in a rage.

II

For a while, in the rocky rubble underfoot, there was nothing at all to follow, for the country was so dry and the sun so hot that even rocks half turned by the pair he had just encountered, if they had in fact come this way, were now as dry and crusty looking as their surroundings. And there was no foliage to have been bruised or to show an upturned leaf. This was a bad stage that could happen, and happen sometimes repeatedly, in any tracking.

So Townsend did the customary thing. In the first place, he had decided definitely before now, that there was a trail of sorts. He proceeded in the straightest possible direction, the general conditions, rocks and little sandstone shards, all general terrain, directing him. Finally he came to a small gulch, probably two spans deep, and its far edge was crumpled, from a passing factory-finished burro shoe.

He saw instantly that this was by far the most satisfactory print he had come across since he had left the water tank, so he dismounted and inspected it painstakingly. The clearest impressions, of course, had been on the damp shore of the creek, but conditions here were unnatural because of the moisture, and the time element was very difficult to estimate. He had come to an opinion, but could hardly believe it.

His inspection now, to his amazement, pretty well confirmed it. The man on the sorrel, with the burro, had passed *within* two days.

Teague's story in Townsend's shack had been a complete lie. He'd said his "son" had been headed for a surveying part forty miles away. That he hadn't shown up and then, after waiting, the party had become alarmed at his non-appearance and sent a runner back. All this was, of course absurd.

Teague had been in hot pursuit.

A little later, Townsend had passed through the rubble, a trail, almost thread-thin and rarely used, and suddenly climbing. There was much sign of the burro and sorrel now, in part-impressions and disturbed leaf mold. Leaf mold, because the lower lip of the timbered mountainside had already begun to engulf him.

The trail, he knew from past experience, long experience, led either over a ridge, or to a far-away gap, or to a possible deeply penetrating valley, and was for the infrequent traveler.

The trail came up into a sort of narrow little tableland, a burn-over, and passed through it into spruce. Townsend wondered, and wondered again, but didn't worry over the kind of situation into which he had so voluntarily placed himself. As long as he was the hound trailing the bear, he knew, he was completely safe. But when the bear became aware of this and turned, it would be a different story. So that was the major element in Townsend's situation, to keep this element concealed.

Beyond the burn-over the trail continued to ascend, but, temporarily at least, at a more gradual slope. He came to, and crossed a cool freshwater stream, about an arms-length wide. This was in itself the seal of the mountain, and its width told him its headwaters would likely come from a nest of grassy springs, high up somewhere.

This would have been a good place to camp for the night, but these were important moments, he knew, if he were to overtake his man and he pushed on briskly.

It was almost sundown, but not quite, and even after sundown there would be a traveling period of afterglow.

There were three people at least in this, he decided, and if there were three there could be more. He watched the signs closely to see if his man on the sorrel was joined by anyone else.

After a bit, the path turned around a thicket of red cedar.

There was a boy in the center of the path. He was about eight years old, scrawny, barefooted, in corduroy pants and apparently nothing else. He was down on his hands and knees, setting the gut loop of a snare directly in the center of the path. Here, thin brush from either side concealed it. A few yards to the left of the trail, the gut was attached to a bent-over sapling.

Townsend came to a halt.

"That looks to me like a rabbit trap," he said.

"It is," bragged the boy. "It isn't generally knowed, but rabbits travel horse trails, too."

"If I was you," said Townsend, "I'd stick to rabbit trails. A rider with a mount he loves isn't going to take kindly to having his mare cut, or even bruised, about the fetlock."

"Then let them watch out for theirselves," said the boy insolently.

"What you going to do if you catch you a sheriff?"

"I'm going to look at him," said the boy. "A sheriff is a rare sight hereabouts."

When Townsend simply munched his empty jaws, the boy said, "How will they know who did it? I'm always somewheres else."

"You know what's going to happen to you, sonny?" said Townsend.

"What?" said the boy defiantly.

"You're going to catch a cow-waddy's horse, and he's going to untangle it, and lead it off the trail, and set back, say in that clump of bushes. And wait."

"And then what?"

"He's going to put those hands of his on you, and beat you half to death."

"But I'm only a boy!" exclaimed the youngster.

"You're going to start out a boy," said Townsend. "But when he gets through thrashing you, you're going to end up a growed man. I guarantee that."

Subdued, the boy took down the snare.

"You mad with me?" asked Townsend, grinning.

"Who wouldn't be?" asked the boy, and then, seeing that there was more to come, added, "Why?"

"Because I was fixing to ask you a favor."

"Well, now, ain't that somethin'," said the boy, but he was interested.

"I want you to tell me how you knew there were rabbits on this trail."

"I've seen them. Many and many a time. Yon's my pap's cabin—past that brush. Don't nothing pass on this trail, from a chipmunk up, but I see him."

And now, with Apache indirectness, Townsend came to his point from an angle, taking the less important thing first. He said, "Did you see two men, one a fat-faced youngish fellow—" and described the two riders who had shot Teague.

"No," said the boy promptly. "They ain't been by, unless they come in the dark o' night, which I doubt, and even then I'd have heard them because I've got a hair-trigger ear."

Now Townsend got to his major interest. He

asked casually, "How about a fellow on a sorrel with a pack burro?"

"Him, yes."

"What did he look like?"

"First we'll take the burro," said the boy. "It was loaded heavy, but not too heavy. A city man loads one with everything but an organ. A trapper or a woodsman loads one entirely different. This one was loaded like the man was bound for a long trip and knew a little but not too much how to handle what he would be up against."

"Now that we've got finished with the burro and it's interestin' pack," said Townsend, wryly amused, but impressed, too, "what about the man on the sorrel. Nothing in detail about the sorrel, please, just the man."

"I'd say he was about forty or maybe a little older," said the boy. "Medium tall, medium heavy-set, medium ugly. Talks with a Texas accent. He was wearing his hat, chin strap around his neck, back off his head between his shoulders. His hair was kind of a carrot red and his sleeves was rolled up and they was fuzzy carrot red hair on his forearms."

"How do you know he spoke with a Texas accent?" asked Townsend. "Did you talk to him?"

"I asked him for a little tobacco for my pipe."

"You mean your pap's pipe."

"I mean *my* pipe, and he said no. How about you?"

"I say no, too," said Townsend. "Do what I did when I was a whippersnapper. Smoke dry weeds. Something I've tried, by the way, in certain desperate circumstances since I've been a man, and mighty unsuccessful. Goodbye."

He started up the trail. Behind him, the boy yelled, "I didn't catch your name."

"You caught me, and my mount, and my pack-horse and its load, down to the smallest button and buckle, I'm sure of that," said Townsend. "That'll have to do."

The trail bent again, and the boy was gone.

About an hour later, the trail passed through a short elongated little hollow. On Townsend's right, in some places overhanging the path, and growing denser and loftier as they dropped way down the mountainside, were hemlocks, knee-high and shoulder-high with underbrush. On his left, the mountain rose steeply, the brush dwindling and becoming patchy and starved on the stone of the earth, showing, too, great lumps of sunset-tinted sandstone and outcrop. He was glancing up the arid slope when the broken iron-weeds caught his attention.

Not more than a dozen all told, and they made a straggling line from the upper heights down the steep slope to a roughish cube of limestone perhaps a hundred yards up.

Just the weeds and the stone, and nothing else.

He slipped from his saddle as innocently as he

could, melted into the underbrush of the hemlocks, recrossed the path. As he had dismounted, in the same casual fluid action, his heavy octagonal-barreled rifle had left its scabbard and become part of him. In a wide circle, he climbed the slope, always covered, almost part of the mountain itself.

When he was above the rock, looking down on it, he saw just exactly what he had expected to see. A man with a gun looking down at his horses. Before him in his stone was a notchlike crevice, scarcely discernable from below; he was peering through this crevice. Now he called down, "Where are you? Come out! I want to ask you something!"

When Townsend failed to respond, he put his rifle to the crevice, sighted carefully, and shot Townsend's packhorse.

He yelled, "Backtrack! Go home! Let that be a warning to you!"

"Turn around!" called Townsend from above him.

The man spun, rifle to his shoulder.

Townsend shot him once, just above the bridge of his nose, and tilted down his heavy 45-70 rifle.

Through thinned lips, in a whisper, he said, "And let that be a warning to you. Killing a man's packhorse! How sorry lowdown can a man get?"

He descended the mountainside leisurely to examine his kill.

III

The dead man was a cow puncher, and one hundred percent cow puncher. He wore tightish legging type chaps of soft leather and a cheap calico shirt, once red probably, now faded to unpleasant orange. His gunbelt was cheap and simple and his six-gun was a cheap flashy rattlesnake killer, nickel plated, the nickel already coming off in patches, with nothing of the professional, even of the expert, about it. His rifle was an ordinary deer rifle, but he sure knew how to use it; the shot hadn't been difficult, but not easy either. In death, he had a gaping unscraped jaw and blobs of dried mucus on his nostril holes.

Townsend searched him. He found a brown staghandled jackknife, a peach seed half carved into a basket—a favorite cowboy pastime—a whistle made of slippery elm bark, probably a dog whistle, and a mess of other typically cowboy odds and ends. He also found a letter, pocket worn, written in pencil and addressed to *Mister John Wilson, Lazy M Ranch, Martinsburg, Idaho.* It was from Kentucky, a mother's letter to her son, giving home gossip, that and nothing else, perfectly genuine, Townsend was convinced, with contents of no significance to him.

Townsend had never heard of any Martinsburg, but that didn't mean anything. When you came right down to it, all this was a foreign land to him.

He made one change before he left the man. He placed the man's gun muzzle in the stone's notch. He was going to leave his slaughtered packhorse exactly as it lay, and the whole picture, to whomever found it later, would give the essentially true version of the ambush. Satisfied, Townsend descended the slope to the trail.

He unpacked the supplies Teague had selected, laid them out in order on the trail, and eventually replaced most of them exactly as they had been. He shook his head at certain luxuries Teague had brought along, three cans of tomatoes and two cans of peaches in syrup, for instance.

The true fact was they weren't mouth-watering to him. His idea of food luxuries were pretty much Apache, kidney fat, for instance, and certain offal which weren't served up to you in restaurants. What he took, after he'd replaced the remainder, was a small skillet, cornmeal, and a chunk of bacon side, about two pounds, which he sliced off neatly with his razor-edged bowie knife.

This done, giving everything—mountainside, notched rock with gun muzzle now glinting in the sun, dead packhorse—a final survey, he mounted his tough little mare and rode on. It was like being home again. No extras, either in humans or packhorses.

Contentedly, he knew now he could make decent time.

And he would have to travel in better time, and in more freedom, too, for obviously the game of secrecy was finished.

Already they, whoever they were, were trying to stop him.

In the days following, he caught up with his target, to about a mile behind him, he judged, and carefully held the distance.

He could easily have overtaken him, but the man himself would hold no answer.

About noon, third day after, he passed a density of young yellow pine, arrow straight, and came into a small cleared area. There was a little parched looking garden enclosed by a primitive settler type brush fence, a low cabin of weather-barked and wind-polished logs, silver bronze in the hammering sunlight, and a lodge-pole corral at the rear.

A trapper's cabin, a nice one, Townsend decided. The tracks he had been trailing turned in here and his eyes narrowed when he glanced at the corral and saw one gray burro and one fine looking sorrel horse. He called, "The house! Hello, the house!"

From where he came from, those who always helloed a lonesome cabin lived the longest. There might be women inside, or there might be a man with a lampblacked gunsight, to whom *everyone* was unwelcome.

To the man who came to the door, however, *everyone* seemed to be welcome. He was a gnarled wizened little man with a short shaggy beard, in filthy bib overalls. He held an open demijohn clasped with both arms to his chest, as tenderly and carefully as though it were a newborn puppy.

He said, "Light and come in, suh. Light and come in. We'uns is jest partakin' o' the fatted calf."

Townsend dismounted, ground-reined his mare, and stepped inside. A man like this he understood. He entered cautiously, though he was sure his quarry was long gone.

He groped his way through the half-light of the windowless room to a table and sat on a thong bottomed stool.

The old man poured him a drink in a handleless teacup and sat opposite him. He said, "My name's Finch. Nice day."

Townsend took a sip from the cup. A trail of fired gunpowder seemed to flash into his throat, explode at the back of his nose, to even explore his ears. He said, "I think it's whiskey."

"It's more'n whiskey," said Mr. Finch proudly. "It's Finch's Special Whiskey. For one thing, it's double run and got more proof than a Canada goose has got pinfeathers. For another, it's got an added something I always put in afterwards so it won't take no back-sass from nobody. I won't tell you what this extra something is, but I'll give you a hint. It kin be found easy on any housewife's kitchen shelf."

"Lye," said Townsend.

"I ain't sayin'. Trade secret."

"And you've added a little barnyard something, too," said Townsend. "For flavor, I'd guess."

"Don't pry," said Mr. Finch.

Around the walls were steel traps, hanging from wooden pegs, and on buckhorns were at least ten rifles, of different calibers.

"Nice looking sorrel and burro in your corral," said Townsend.

"Ain't they, though," said Mr. Finch. "I got 'em on a mighty good swap. Traded a feller my old bay for 'em, for both. Scarcely two hour ago. He was in desperate circumstances."

"How come desperate?" asked Townsend.

"A feller was trailing him, you I think."

Townsend said nothing.

Mr. Finch said, "I'll have to tell you I don't hold with one feller trailin' another. It hain't mannerly, for one thing. I've had it happen to me in days long gone, and it always made me nervous."

"Show me which way he went, and point out this bay's tracks to me," said Townsend.

"Can't. I promised not to. That was part of the

swap. The main part. He's a-tryin' to befuddle you, you see," added Mr. Finch patiently.

"Scarcely two hours ago?" said Townsend.

"That's right. Sat right there in the same stool you're sittin' on, and drank from the same cup. You might even be drinking his dregs, but what sensible man is goin' to be fussy about a little thing like that?"

"I hate to tell you," said Townsend politely. "It's going to make it a little harder, but I don't need your help. I'll just look around outside until I find your bay's tracks. I can tell 'em because she must have left a million of them, and just start off again where I left off, this time after the bay."

"What you and this other party been up to?"

Townsend didn't answer.

"Do you think you're smarter'n me?" asked Mr. Finch amiably.

"No, sir," said Townsend courteously. "I sure wouldn't say that."

"Then don't waste your time. I wrapped my bay's feet in thick burlap, led her out to a certain tree, and the gentleman—"

"The red-haired Texan?"

"I didn't say that. The gentleman took off his boots and carried them and went out to her."

"And you think all that nonsense can't be tracked as easy as factory-finished horse shoes?" asked Townsend.

Mr. Finch looked annoyed.

But the truth was, time, time, time. It would take a lot of time. Maybe too much.

More and more, Townsend was getting the feeling that the element of time in this could be a crisis.

He decided to short-cut, to pass up the red-haired man for the time being and turn his attention to this John Wilson of the Lazy M ranch, the man who had wanted to stop him, to kill him, and had killed his packhorse maliciously as a substitute.

He said to Mr. Finch, "What is your opinion of me, personal?"

"I'm drinkin' with you, hain't I? And I sure as hell don't drink with ever'body."

"Then answer me a few questions, and not about your horse swap. Do you know a chubby faced young man that goes around at times with a bug-eyed man that's got yellow teeth like pumpkin seeds?" He went on to describe the men that had gunned down Teague, in detail. Bobbie and his pal.

"Never seen nor heard o' either of 'em, thank goodness. They sure don't sound appetizing."

"How do I get to Martinsburg?" asked Townsend.

"Well," said Mr. Finch. "You can't miss it. You jest go along the path you been follerin'. In two days you'll come to the Lazy M Ranch. You cross the ranch and in a day or so more you'll hit Martinsburg, or, if you're like me, it'll hit you."

"How about this Lazy M outfit. Are they hard on wandering trespassers?"

"They're free and easy. Mr. Teague is free and easy about ever'thing."

"Mr. Teague?" said Townsend. "You mean Mr. Joe Teague?"

"No, I mean Mr. Alfred Teague, the Lazy M owner."

Townsend described the man who had hired him.

"Lawsy no," said Mr. Finch. "Not in any particular. And I mean physical particular, so I'm sure. Clothes don't count. They can be put on and took off so you can't say yes or no who is a man by his clothes. But you can by his physical. The man you're talking about ain't an inhabitant of this part of the country, and never has been since I can remember, and I'm certain of that. You're a careful talker and I'm a careful listener and I'm mighty certain."

"And you've seen them all?" said Townsend skeptically.

"I think I can say yes to that," said Mr. Finch. "In my goings and comings, all. And I don't relish sourcasm."

"Well, I'll be getting along," said Townsend, arising. "As you'll notice, I've left a few dregs in my cup myself, for your next visitor. Thank you for your hospitality."

"Goodbye," said Mr. Finch. "It was a pleasure meetin' you. If I don't see you again, live a long and joyous life, like me."

He camped that night, out of sight and sound of the trail, away to one side behind a tangle of briars and grapevines, in a pocket of grass, his horse on a long picket rope. She was as accustomed to the trail as he was; she got grain when it was naturally and financially obtainable, and the rest of the time made out like Townsend, always equally good and a little better, he saw to that. But you couldn't always choose. The things he could control, he did. He never overrode her, never pushed her as hard as he pushed himself. He never tossed a coin to see whether she got grain or he got ham and eggs.

Next morning the trail climbed steeply, eventually topping a low place in a ridge, as he had long ago suspected it might. There was tamarack here, at first in a straggly belt, and then, as the path descended, the trees gave way to very rough traveling indeed—scarp, and rocky chasms, and now and then a great monolith. Then came a patch of springs and tall coarse grass, the headwaters to a creek, he knew, and then the creek itself, flowing downward, hardly three fingers wide at this high-level stage.

By noon he was in the great pine forest, the mountain covering you always saw from far below.

He was just finishing his lunch in the saddle, cold corn dodger and bacon, remnants of his breakfast's campfire, when the trees parted momentarily and gave him a vista of a beautiful valley below him.

There was a clump of buildings, ranch buildings, and as far as his eye could reach, to the left and right of them, were pale green emerald swales speckled with countless cattle.

He touched his mare lightly on her flanks and she continued picking her way downward through the blanket of pine needles.

It was about four-thirty that afternoon, and the dust motes were a lemon-yellow haze in the lower air, when he rode up to the rack before the ranch house-office, dismounted, and paused a moment, looking around.

The building before him was two storied at one end, with a cupola and weather vane, and with a one-story lateral annex. A veranda stretched down its full length, and the whole thing looked like what it was, part residence, part business headquarters. Behind it, on either side, scattered, were the workshops and barns and corrals. Beyond the barn, a new silver gleaming windmill turned sleepily.

He mounted a step at the lower end, the one-story end, and knocked at a door marked office. A genial voice called, “Come in!”

Inside, he found himself in a bare hot room, with cobwebs like fishnets on the ceiling corners. There were three or four chairs, a big brass spittoon about the size of a floral urn in the middle of a pine floor, and a man at a dining room table desk set against a wall, beneath a hanging frame of pigeonholes, well stuffed. There was a frog in a half-filled goldfish bowl, and the man was trying to feed it as it sat on its rock, trying to feed it with a cracker he was crumbling. “Army hardtack,” he said to Townsend. “That’s what he thrives on best of all. Just good old U.S. Army hardtack. I don’t believe I know you. Just pull up a chair and sit down.”

He was a short energetic man, with glazed inflamed rims to his eyelids, and a mouth he couldn’t have made unfriendly if he tried. Townsend liked him on sight. He liked him so much he became suddenly suspicious of his judgement. He said, “I’m Mark Townsend. Who do I have the pleasure of addressing?” He got it off without too much flourish, and was proud of it. He was trying to be decently companionable, if he had to fall over backwards.

The short man coughed, then grinned. “I haven’t heard such an elegant sentence since I was a boy. I know damn well you’re not a cow-hand from your clothes. You dress more like a trapper. Don't tell me you're a school teacher in disguise?"

Townsend laughed. "I picked it up somewhere and it jest slipped out."

"I'm Alf Teague," said the man. "The owner here."

"I once heard of a Mr. Joe Teague," said Townsend. "Any kin?"

"Joe Teague was my brother," said Teague, and his face, to Townsend's surprise, went pretty bleak and flinty. "From my point of view, he's dead."

"Sorry to hear it," said Townsend, looking mildly attentive.

"He left our hearth and home and broke my mother's heart when he was sixteen. Became a gambler, I've since heard. First a backroom pool parlor gambler, then a tent gambler at fairs and such, and ended up a saloon gambler down in Colorado. He's written me now and then, but I never answer. He broke my mother's heart."

"And as far as you're concerned, he's dead."

"That's right. Okay if we don't talk about him? What can I do for you?"

"Need a wolfer on this place?" asked Townsend.

"So that's what you are, a wolfer," said Teague. "I was pretty close in my guess, wasn't I? No, I'm sorry but we don't."

Townsend didn't take it too kindly. So that's what he looked like up here in the north to an

Idaho rancher? A wolfer. Wolfers were for the most part, in his opinion, drifting scum who couldn't do anything else—and looked it.

"Then I'll be getting along," said Townsend. "And thank you for your time. But just one thing more."

"Yes?"

"My papa had a double cousin twice removed who had a son from Kentucky that somebody or other said might work somewheres around here."

As he talked, Townsend saw again that mountainside, and the man he had shot, dead at his feet, behind the rock.

"What was his name?" asked Teague.

"Name of John Wilson," said Townsend. "Was a hand, I think I heard, at an outfit named the Lazy M."

"This is the Lazy M," said Teague. "And a John Wilson, from Kentucky, is my foreman."

"A good one?"

"Good? I'll say good. I don't believe we could get along without him."

Townsend had to say something. So he said, "How do I find my way to Martinsburg?"

IV

That night he camped by simply curling up and making himself a rabbit's nest in the sweet-smelling prairie grass.

All day next day it was prairie, rising and falling, with the great mountains flanking his shoulder. Prairie and mountains seemed endless. This night, the second night, he camped in the shelter of aspens, along a clear, chill stream and caught a tiny flopping minnow in his hat when he took his after-supper drink of water.

About noon he came to railroad tracks, extending forward and behind in a tiny diminishing ladder. And not long after, he came to cattle chutes, and a hodgepodge maze of feeder pens. Then came an expanse, narrow and irregular of weedy vacant lots, and the furthermost outskirts of the town.

Here it was huts, cottages, and shanties, mainly, widely scattered. Most with makeshift privies and poor excuses for garden patches.

His direction, however, took him past a neat sheathed cabin with a fastidious garden and a thumbnail corral beside a good barn. A sad-faced middle aged man in misshapen pants and a generously ripped shirt was standing at a corral, petting a calico foal. His short boots were worn and ankle-turned. His pants, sagging on his hip-bones, seemed almost slipping off. Townsend, interested in the foal, came to a halt.

Now, close up, the man looked a little, well, hardcase.

They stared at each other, and nodded formally.

"Mighty nice lookin' little mare," said the man, pointing at Townsend's mount. "What do you call her?"

"Star," said Townsend.

"Star?" said the man, frowning. "I don't see no blaze."

"Full name's Evening Star."

"Oh," said the man wisely. "Called after some special little Indian girl, maybe."

Then the man said a surprising thing. He said steadily, "You shouldn't have left her."

"I didn't," said Townsend quietly. "She left me. She was Apache, killed by a Comanche arrow."

The man nodded very gently. He said, "I won't trouble you to tell you I'm a heap sorry."

"I was just admiring your calico foal," said Townsend, pointedly changing the subject. "I like her nature."

"You don't give a growed horse a good nature with a braided rawhide quirt," said the man. "You bring it on foal-size with human decency. By the way, my name is Holgate. Care to get down and have a cup of coffee?"

"I'd like to, but I'm in a hurry," said Townsend. "I'm Mark Townsend."

"Come from over the mountains?"

"Is it any of your affair?"

"Yes. Because I want to look under your saddle."

Townsend permitted him to feel under his saddle blanket. He could sense groping, stroking fingers over his mare.

Holgate said, "Beginnings of saddle sore. Not sore, just the beginning so far."

He went into the house and came out with a quart purple-colored, long-necked wine bottle. He took some of the solution it contained in the palm of his hand and rubbed it under the saddle. "Feels like a bruise so far, nothing else. Now I make this purely myself. Melted rosin and bees-wax and spirits of turpentine, among other things, but mainly it's the way you cook it and stir it."

He glanced at the mare's flank. "Why, they's a scratch here!" he exclaimed.

"It just a briar scratch," said Townsend.

"Flies lays eggs in any kind of a scratch," said Holgate. He coated it with a little ointment. "This keeps away flies, too. And is wonderful for such a purpose alone, when a horse is new gelded."

Townsend thanked him, and started to ride away. He stopped. "How much do I owe you?" he asked.

"For what?" asked Holgate.

Suddenly an idea hit Townsend. He said, "I'm

going to be in town, I don't know how long. I don't much care for the way some livery stables treat a fellow's mount. Would you, personal, right here, board and take care of my mare for me?"

"Nothing could give me more pleasure," said Holgate.

Townsend dismounted, handed Holgate the reins and started away.

"Whoa!" called Holgate.

Townsend came to a halt and turned.

"Where you goin' to stable yourself?" asked Holgate.

"Some hotel or rooming house, I guess," said Townsend. "I don't know."

"Why not take a stall and manger with me?" said Holgate. "As my guest. And before you say no, let me put it this way. I'm mighty lonesome."

"But I don't know when I'll be in, and I don't know when I'll be out. And I may come running in some dawn with buckshot buzzing around my ears."

"All the better," said Holgate, placidly.

Grinning, Townsend walked up to him and shook his hand. He hadn't shaken hands a half dozen times in the past five years. The iron clasp he got in return was like a pair of pliers.

"Need anything?" asked Holgate mildly.

"Plenty," said Townsend. "But I don't know what. I'll see you later."

Behind him, as he left, Holgate yelled, "What shall I do with your 45-70?"

"Just treat it like you treat your foal," called Townsend. "With human decency."

The town, when Townsend got into the heart of it, proved to be of considerable size, with a population of maybe twelve hundred. He had anticipated as much when he passed those loading chutes. You didn't really judge a town by its resident population alone. It could be the market center, and shipping center for as many as three counties.

He saw it was just a cattle-railroad town like a good many others he'd seen, except for one thing. There was the row of shops and offices and saloons, brick and frame, one and two and even three stories along Main Street, and the boardwalk of different levels with extended wooden billboards here and there along it, and the spaced timber stile-like stepdowns to the road. The road, as usual, was wide and rutted, here and there deeply so. At the far edge of the road, however, was a sort of gully about five feet deep, with sloping sides and a stream at the bottom. Now, in the dry season, the stream was just a trickle but there would be times, he knew, when it would churn past full to the brim. Up and down the street, he could see three wagon-wide, heavy-plank bridges over the gully.

Beyond the creek was the railroad, and beyond

the tracks and station he could see other houses and saloons and shops, jumbled, and seedy looking. Every cattle town had one of these neighborhoods, too.

Where a sign said *Wells Fargo*, he stopped in and had one of Joe Teague's gold pieces changed into smaller and more convenient legal tender. He then sought out a restaurant, a hole in the wall called simply, *Slim's*, sat at the counter and, reading one of the many placards on the wall, ordered chitterings and cabbage. When the waiter-owner, stubbled-faced and bleary-eyed, placed the meal before him, he waited until he had received his pay, and tucked the money away, and then said, "Excuse me, but I allus shut my eyes when a customer orders and eats that stuff. I wouldn't even stock it, but we got a lot of Dixie boys in town and they demands it. You know what it is?"

Townsend, amused, ate silently and with relish.

The counterman said, "Them's intestines, hog guts. I can scarcely bring myself to cook 'em."

"Ever eat antelope eyeballs?" asked Townsend.

"You must excuse me," said the counterman. "I got things to do in the kitchen."

As Townsend left the restaurant, a man standing just outside the door touched him lightly, almost hesitantly, and Townsend turned.

The man was portly, over-plump with a protruding stomach, and shiny cheeks a heart-attack red. When he began to speak, his voice was deep but affable. If there was any way Townsend would have described him, he would have said fatherly. He was about the most fatherly acting and talking human Townsend had ever encountered.

" 'Evening," said the portly man. "Do I know you?"

"No," said Townsend.

"I'm Sheriff Purdy," said the man. "I got my badge on me someplace. Care to see it?"

"Don't bother," said Townsend.

"It's not much to look at anyway," said the sheriff sadly. "You know I hear some men, someplaces, have gold ones, and they're not even sheriffs. Honorary sheriffs. I guess you've got to be honorary to rate gold." A little ice came into his voice. "Care to go over to that bench and talk a little?"

"If you say so," said Townsend.

"It don't look too comfortable," said the sheriff. "But it's the best I see."

It was all too gentle, too paternal.

When they had seated themselves on a bench before a saddler's, the sheriff said, "They's a button missing from your jacket."

"I know," said Townsend. "Is it agin the law here?"

"No, of course not. And my wife would say your shirt is very poorly patched."

"I know. I'm a bachelor. Is there a law agin that, too?"

"That's a double question," said Sheriff Purdy. "You mean the bachelor part or the patch?"

"Either?"

"Neither. What I'm getting at is, Bert Ellison, over at Wells Fargo was just saying he changed a twenty-dollar gold piece for you. Gold pieces are like eggs. You hardly ever just find one in a basket alone. How come you're so poor in your clothes, and so rich in your pockets."

"Maybe I'm a hoarder," said Townsend. "A miser."

"That won't do," said the sheriff, showing a little of that metal again.

"Well, I didn't steal it," said Townsend. "Is that what you want to know?"

"Yes. Among other things. What's your name?"

Townsend told him.

"Where are you from?" asked the sheriff.

Townsend told him about San Carlos, and his failure to hold ranching jobs.

The sheriff listened with interest, and suddenly with understanding and sympathy, it seemed to Townsend.

"Where are you staying?" asked the sheriff. "The Rooming House or the Hotel?"

"I scarcely know," said Townsend. "I haven't been on Main Street twenty minutes."

"Lookin' for work?"

Townsend told him about applying at Lazy M as wolfer, and being turned away.

"You don't look like a wolfer to me," said the sheriff. "And not going around changing twenty-dollar gold pieces, too. I might add."

Townsend said nothing.

"Alf Teague is not taking on any strangers these days," said the sheriff. "He's got rustler trouble."

"I didn't know that," said Townsend.

"Down there where you come from," said the sheriff, "a good deal of rustling is taking a herd, or half a herd, or a third, or as many as you can handle, cross the line into Mexico where you're safe. We have our share of that, too. Cross the mountains to Wyoming or Montana, or up into Canada. But our main nuisance is just a few, now and then. Right now a cow is worth twenty dollars at the chutes. If this kind of stealing is done systematic on big herds, at twenty dollars per, it can run into sizable amounts and I mean sizable."

"What's he doing to stop it?" asked Townsend.

"A few, now and then, but systematic is mighty hard to stop," said the sheriff. "Why did you suddenly start to lie to me?"

"What do you mean?"

"I mean you're no wolfer and money couldn't pay you to strychnine an animal to death. You'd just cut his throat with that handmade bowie o' yours."

"Do you question all strangers this way?" asked Townsend.

"Have to. We get some mighty desperate characters sometimes."

Shocked, Townsend said, "You mean you think I might be a desperate character!"

"I don't know what *you* think you are," said the sheriff, "but messing around with renegade Apache war parties is something I don't even want my peace-loving mind to ponder."

A man rode by on a bay, about the saddest bag of bones and horsemeat Townsend had ever seen. The man in the saddle was average tall, cowboy dressed but travelworn, red-haired with fuzzy pink hair on his forearms. His hat was slung back on its leather chin strap and hung between his shoulders. His face was certainly medium ugly, at least.

It was the man the boy had described, Townsend somehow felt, and the poor old bay was the nag Mr. Finch had traded to him for a pack-laden burro and a good sorrel. This, Townsend was sure, was the man Joe Teague had originally paid him to track. He was as sure of this, as if he were listening to the man speak in a Texas accent.

Not far down the street was a low white picket fence and a big sign which overhung the sidewalk. The sign said: Rooming House. The man dismounted, tied his bay, and went through the picket gate.

Well, thought Townsend, *I've earned my money. I've got him.*

Sheriff Purdy asked, "Ever been inside a jail?"

"Who hasn't?" said Townsend. "We all have friends, don't we?"

"Ever been arrested?"

"No," said Townsend.

"Well, keep it that way," said the sheriff cheerfully. "Goodbye." He left.

Townsend walked down the street and passed through the white picket gate.

A dowdy little woman with a starched apron answered when he clanged the hand-pull doorbell. He said, "I'm just a visitor. I'd like a few words with our red-haired Texas friend."

"You mean Mr. Red River?" said the landlady. "Go right up those stairs. Second door to your left."

The stairs were narrow and steep, covered with moldy drab carpet supposed, Townsend decided, to give it a homelike touch. He passed the tiny upstairs landing and knocked on a cheap pine door, unseasoned and warped, and thinly mahogany-stained. The china doorknob turned, the door opened, and he found himself facing a medium-big man, a little more than medium-ugly, squint-eyed, red-haired, bulbous-jawed, with a cluster of scabs under his left earlobe. In a Texas voice, the man said, "What do you want."

He managed to make it mighty insulting, the way he said it.

"In," said Townsend shortly.

"Who in the hell are you?" asked the man.

"I'm the man who has been tracking you," said Townsend.

"So you're the one," said the man, tonelessly.

"All the way across the mountains from the water tank," said Townsend.

"So you're the one," said the man, in a snarl that showed not his lips, but the gums of his lower teeth.

"Right."

"Why?"

"Well, not just to look at you," said Townsend, that old uncontrollable black rage coming over him again, just for an instant. "The sight would be scarcely worth the trip."

After a pause, the Texan said, "Come in."

V

Townsend walked in.

When he had been put together, fear had been left out of his makeup. When he walked in, he walked like the Texan was the visitor here, not himself.

It was a small food-smelling room with a brass bedstead, walls papered with mildewed trumpet vines and hummingbirds, and a meagerness of other cheap furniture. Townsend sat on a chair and Red River leaned against the door jamb, his hand loosely by his gunbutt. He wore his gun hipbone high, cowboy style, not low slung and fancy, gunman style.

He looked to Townsend as mean as a tarantula, but he wasn't a professional gunfighter, Townsend was certain of that. That didn't mean he couldn't be a hundred percent butcher, of course. You didn't have to be a gunman to be a killer.

"They told me someone was houndin' me," said Red River insolently. "And all it comes down to is you."

"That's right," said Townsend blandly, now again under control. "Just me."

There was a moment silence.

Then Townsend said, "Who told you? How did you get this information?"

"You know how it is, a feller picks up things here and there. Well, here I am. What do you want?"

"I was paid a hundred dollars to carry you a message."

Red River looked alert and interested. "From who?"

"From Mr. Teague."

"Mr. Alf Teague?" asked Red River, looking confused.

Townsend said, "No. From Mr. Joe Teague."

"I don't know any Mr. Joe Teague."

"Then you'll never know him," said Townsend sadly. "A couple of funny robbers killed him and then forgot to rob him."

"What was the message?" asked Red River carelessly.

"I wasn't paid a hundred dollars to give it to just anyone," said Townsend reasonably. "Who you care to identify, even just a little?"

Red River looked torn with doubt. Finally, he said, "I'm a cowhand from Colorado. Does that check?" Townsend nodded. "I'm from a spread just now outside of town. Mr. Alf Teague's. Starting tomorrow, I'm his new foreman."

Townsend said, "But I talked to him this afternoon. He said he was happy, and more than happy with the foreman he has now, name of John Wilson, I believe."

"He's heard information since then. John Wilson fell off his horse and kilt hisself quite a piece down the trail, and Mr. Teague has jest heard."

"And the job was open, and you stepped into it," said Townsend.

"That's right."

"Pretty good luck, hey?"

"Oh, I'd have got work of some kind at the Lazy M anyways," said Red River. He was bragging, but Townsend felt there was a ring of truth in it, too. "I come highly recommended. Now what was that message?"

Townsend said, speaking slowly, dramatically, "I was to tell you: The old blueback primer was right; *Take one teaspoonful ever three hours.*"

"I don't think that's from no blueback primer," said Red River, puzzled. "It sounds like a label on a medicine bottle. And I ain't sick."

"I don't know."

"What's it mean to you?"

"Nothing."

"But you crossed a ridge of the Bitteroots, and he paid you a hundred dollars."

"That's right."

Townsend got up to leave. At the door he stopped, at first impelled to ask about a Bobbie and a pair of Apache moccasins, then deciding not to rush things.

Neither of them bothered to indicate a polite parting as he left.

The windows of Holgate's little cottage glowed

soft golden in the purple of the dusty twilight as Townsend returned to it. He had made a careful but casual seeming search of the town, saloons, stores, sidewalk benches, and had seen nothing that looked like Bobbie or his friend, or an Apache moccasin with an upturned toe. He knocked on Holgate's door, was summoned in, and entered.

He stepped into a small front room, and had to grin at it. Slick yellow furniture, cheap brightly-colored carpet, a cabinet in a corner with knicknacks, a boy-tall vase of artificial flowers in a corner. Holgate's voice had come from an open door at the rear. Newspapers were laid over the carpet from the front door to this door. It was a room right out of the window of a store, a room assembled by a man who wanted a respectable home, a room that had never been lived in, and, by golly, never would be. Townsend decided from now on always to enter the house by the rear, through the kitchen.

"Back here!" called Holgate.

Townsend walked across the newspaper and entered the kitchen.

This was more like it.

It was a kitchen, all right, with clapboard walls, but somehow put Townsend in mind of a line camp. Holgate, stripped to the waist as though he were driving railroad spikes, stood over a range, frying mush.

"Supper," he said. "This ain't as quite as fancy as the Busy Bee in town. Truth is, I seem to like eating better than I do cooking, so probably it won't be nothing to go crazy over."

Townsend, ravenously hungry, couldn't help glancing into the huge iron skillet. In the center of the skillet was a big flat patty of mush and circling it was a big loop of cased sausage, spluttering to drive a waiting man wild with starvation. He judged there must be about three pounds each of sausage and mush.

"No greens," said Holgate. "And without greens, o' course, you get scrofula."

"I like scrofula," said Townsend. "I like it almost as well as I do sausage and mush. And while I'm on the subject, I hate to upset such a satisfactory status quo, but if you really hate cooking, I can take over, starting tomorrow."

"I'm afraid to trust you," said Holgate. "How do I know you won't be wasteful?"

They ate at the oilcloth-covered table. When they had finished, they lolled back in their chairs, which took quite a technique as they were straight backed and straight legged, and each put fire to tobacco.

Townsend said dreamily, "I feel it coming on that I'm going to tell you the story of why I'm sitting here in your house."

"That's up to you," said Holgate contentedly. "Which story you going to tell?"

"How about the true one?" said Townsend.

"Suit yourself," said Holgate mildly.

"Well, I was born a boy in the Tombigbee swamp in Alabama," said Townsend.

"When you tell a story, you sure tell it," said Holgate. "Which I approve of."

"Then we went to Arizona," said Townsend. "I started out with the regulation family, little girl, little boy, one mamma, one papa, and ended up in an Apache village, nobody but me, at a feast over our family ox, braves and squaws squabbling over my parents' clothes."

Stoney-faced, Holgate nodded.

"I learned English at the beginning from half-bloods, later at a mission school, and polished it to its present perfection from the U.S. Cavalry."

"But you'd learned other things in the mean-time," said Holgate.

"A few," said Townsend modestly.

Then came the San Carlos guide and tracker part, the whim to come north to Idaho, the being fired repeatedly for not being companionable. Finally, Indian style, obliquely, he came to the Joe Teague part, Bobbie and the stolen moccasins, and the trip over the ridge; this part he told in painstaking detail, trying to leave nothing out. You either trusted a man, or you didn't, and he trusted Holgate completely. Finally, he told about Red River and the rooming house, and Holgate smiled, and became grave.

Townsend said, "And now Sheriff Purdy kind of lets drop that the Lazy M is losing cows, persistent."

"Yes, indeed. It's a scandal."

"Any ideas on the subject?"

"Me?" said Holgate. "No, sirree. None whatso-ever!"

He fooled around the room for a while, and at last came up with a pencil stub and a scrap of dirty paper.

"If you're aimin' to be around for a while, you should know the general layout of the country," he said. "I thought I'd just sketch you a rough map."

"I'd thank you for same," said Townsend.

Deftly, Holgate made two ovals in the center of the paper, like chain links, one quite large, one much smaller.

"These, both of 'em together is Lazy M," he said. "The big one here, out in front, is the one you visited, Lazy M proper. The smaller one, back here, is also part of Teague's spread but they call it Spruce Pasture, because it's hemmed in, in a kind of rough way by mountainsides and hit-and-miss spruce. Teague keeps a handful of cows here, his best and fattest, but it's behind the house, and behind the big herd out front, and hard to get to. Nothing is ever took from it. His trouble is from cows that just seem to vanish from the big herd—and do I mean big—out front."

Just north of when the two valleys joined, where the two chain links seemed to touch, he made a little cross. He then crumpled the paper and put it in the range and waited until it was consumed by fire.

"What did the little cross mean?" asked Townsend.

"Where the two valleys joined? Just north? Nothing. I didn't know I put one down."

"Well, you sure did."

"That's where a rancher named Blatchford lives. He's got a sizable outfit himself. But nothing to do with what we're talking about."

Staring at the diamond pattern in the oilcloth, Townsend said, "I have a feeling you haven't spent your whole life in Sunday School."

"Where I've been and what I've did," said Holgate placidly, "I'm putting in quite a little will power to forgit."

"I'm going to ask your opinion on one thing," said Townsend. "And I'd appreciate your judgment on it. Why do you think this Joe Teague was paying me to catch this Red River and catch up with him?"

"I can only give you the idea that strikes me."

"That's what I'm asking for."

"Say this Joe Teague, a gambler you was told, was sitting in a faro or poker game in some saloon down in Colorado, and in the chit-chat coming over the table he heard this Red River, maybe drunk, expostulatin' on a new job he just got, and how them cows was took up at the Lazy M. Maybe this Joe Teague was more of a brother to Alf than Alf thought. Maybe he come to a decision to step in and take matter into his own hands, and headed up here to Idaho after Red River to threw a wrench in their works."

When Townsend listened calm faced, Holgate said, "And they stopped him. He was stopped."

"He was stopped," said Townsend. "I fell down on my job."

"That ain't no sane way of looking at it."

"I took his money," said Townsend. "And I'm going to keep it."

"Naturally."

"But I'm not no thief," said Townsend. "I'm going to earn it."

"You stay away from Bill Blatchford," ordered Holgate. "And you stay away from Alf Teague."

"Why do you link them together?" asked Townsend.

"I link 'em apart," said Holgate. "They hate each other. You get caught between them and you're caught between a couple of mighty powerful millstones."

Holgate yawned, putting a little too much into it. "They's a cot in the corner. That's your'n. I'll sleep on a buffalo hide pallet."

"I'll sleep on the buffalo hide," said Townsend. "I want to get a good night's sleep."

"I always strive to give a guest what he so desires," said Holgate.

Townsend glanced around. His octagonal barreled 45-70 was on stag's antlers above the back door.

"If you hear that thing being lifted from its prongs before daylight," said Townsend, gesturing, "just turn over and go back to sleep."

"You're headin' for one of Tony Antonelli's cheap-priced but loving-cut ornamental headstones," said Holgate. "But I guess it's up to you."

VI

It was pitch black when Townsend woke up, dressed, and took down his rifle, but the feel of moisture and chill on his skin, and the smell of things, told him it was just before dawn, as surely as if he had a gold engraved watch. He ate his breakfast at the range from the skillet, a chunk of cold greasy mush, a piece of cold greasy sausage, and he had never tasted anything better. He found the barn in the blackness outside without any trouble, and Star easily, as he had so many times before, by simply exchanging good morning with her.

He found corn, put some in her manger, and waited patiently as she chomped kernels from cob. He touched three saddles with his fingertips, located his own by the scratch on its skirt, saddled up, led Star outside and watered her. With the 45-70 securely in its boot, he left town, directing himself north through the fragrant dewy prairie grass by the glinting stars in the ebony sky.

Dawn came, first dove gray behind slender cloud streamers, and then with a fierce red sun that burned the streamers away and paled to intense brassy heat. By this time he was in Lazy M's big lower valley, threading his way through countless cattle. He saw no sign of any human, only cows. For a while he amused himself deciding which of them he would steal if he were an Apache, which if he were a rustler, and which if he simply wanted a steak.

It looked almost, as though he could have taken the lot, for that matter, and made his choice somewhere else, at his leisure.

The first man he saw, he saw next morning, shortly after he had broken his night's camp.

In fact he saw four of them, sitting behind the Lazy M bunkhouse, playing cards, or just digesting their breakfasts, or something—certainly not working.

He made it a point of passing the ranch buildings at a distance, and was certain he was not seen himself.

When the sun at his left was about three quarters of the way down the western sky, the valley suddenly contracted in forested knobs, seeming at first to come to a dead end. He halted his mount, and surveyed the landscape. There must be a passage through these knobs, he knew from Holgate's map, probably zigzag and weaving, and beyond must lay Spruce Pasture, the smaller valley, the valley with the never-stolen choice cattle.

He turned and studied the west. Here were knobs, too, humpy and a little bigger and desolate. At their base, however, he saw a line of cottonwoods, arrow straight, beautifully and evenly spaced, and of almost uniform size. Cottonwoods only grew this way naturally under one condition—along a freshwater stream. And such a stream would have no origin in the valley floor; such a stream would be born from beyond the uplands he was staring at, the hem of uplands on the north. And such a stream, so straight, meant it was a stream of great age, which meant long time erosion, which meant it had long ago carved out a path for itself, something, possibly a chaotic ravine, possibly, even, a little feeder valley, very diminutive; its way out.

Its way out for itself, a way in for others.

Townsend rode to the cottonwoods and examined the stream. If its flow was rushing, turbulent, its backtrack would be craggy, steep. If its flow was slow, the grade of its backtrack would be almost negligible. Its flow was very slow indeed. From that, Townsend decided it simply flowed from some other valley floor to the north.

From a hidden spur valley which must certainly be Blatchford's.

Townsend began to follow it, upstream. He went east for about a mile along the fringe of the foothill slopes, and then the stream turned right, north, around a sparkling granite bluff which even over eons it had been unable to erode. Before long it made a second turn, a great meandering S turn, and Townsend found himself in scrubby brushy flats. Soon the flats opened onto a rolling plain, cattle spotted, and enclosed with the smoky green teeth of mountains. Close by, a straggling group of ranch buildings glowed, coral and gold, in the setting sun. It was a nice-looking outfit, peaceful and serene from the near distance, but when the rider came out to meet him, low in the saddle and with a good more speed than was necessary, he began to wonder.

And when the rider slewed up to a skidding stop before him, blocking him, and he got a look at the rider, he wondered no more. He was a tough little character, with eyes about as lifelike as oil scum, and with his pistol thonged just above his right knee joint.

The rider said, "Brother, this a spread knowed as the W Bar B. When we want visitors, we send out fancy invitations. I say you're trespassin', what do you say?"

"I say get your saddle away from my mare's belly before I tear your head off," said Townsend.

The man looked thoughtful, and backed away a pace, not far but he backed.

He asked, "What are you doing here?"

"I want to talk to Mr. Blatchford," said Townsend.

"Why?"

"Are you Mr. Blatchford? If not, I can't see it's any of your business."

"This way," said the man. "And ride about ten feet ahead o' me."

"With you so curdled?" said Townsend. "Not likely. We'll just ride stirrup to stirrup."

The man studied him, gauged him, and said, "All right. Move!"

Blatchford sat on the narrow-railed porch of his vertical-planked ranch house home, with a sticky coal-black cigar in one hand and bottle of beer in the other, his feet out before him, taking a few minutes pre-supper relaxation. Townsend's companion cantered up. Townsend slipped from his mare Indian fashion, and tied her to a big iron ring set in a heavy post.

Blatchford, only faintly interested, stared at him. He stared back.

First, looking at the man, Townsend saw the X Holgate had drawn so unnecessarily on the map, and then he saw the Bill Blatchford that everyone else saw.

Deeply tanned, middle-aged, weather whipped, thoughtful of lip and level gazed, he looked all cattleman. He held his cigar reversed, its ash and ember within the cup of his palm, as he had learned to protect it so many times, doubtless, against a prairie gale.

When he spoke, his voice was neither cordial nor hostile. He said, "Something on your mind?"

"I want a job as a wolfer," said Townsend.

"I don't need a wolfer," said Blatchford, now

mildly affable. "And where, may I ask, is your wagon?" A wolfer's cart was almost his home.

"I lost it in a poker game," said Townsend.

"In a poker game with some other wolfers," said Blatchford, dreamily. "Now there would be a sight to observe."

"So I have to have a new job to get a new wagon," said Townsend.

"That's understandable," said Blatchford, and lapsed into silence.

Finally, he said, "You asked at Alf Teague's, and he said no, too, eh?"

"That's right," said Townsend.

"Alf and me are not the best of friends," said Blatchford, incidentally.

"What I was thinking about," said Townsend, "was how you knew I'd been there. You know what I think? I think you'd get a pretty good view of the Lazy M ranch house from the top of that bluff with a pair of strong field glasses. Do you watch it?"

"A sensible man watches everything. It's an interestin' world."

"Interesting house, and interesting Front Pasture herd."

"Yes."

"Especially the herd."

"Yes."

"Does he do that to you?" asked Townsend, curiously. "Do all the folks in this part of Idaho do that? Climb a tree or a bluff with a pair of field glasses?"

"Put it this way," said Blatchford expressionlessly. "If somebody could catch some larcenous somebody else down in the Lazy M Front Pasture, doin' some separatin', and brought same to public knowledge, a lot of unpleasantness would evaporate around here."

And a man with a good pair of field glasses, if *he* happened to be a little larcenous minded, might find it amusing to judge the lean from the fat, Townsend decided.

He said, "I consider you a fairly good judge of character."

"Well, thank you," said Blatchford. "But I don't really see no need for you to put it so strong."

"I consider you a fairly good judge of character. Would you add me up as a man who could keep his own counsel?"

"I'd figure you to be downright close-mouthed, if you had a mind to be."

"Then answer me this. Are you expecting a range war?"

Blatchford turned to stone. "Range war?" he said. "What on earth gave you such an outlandish notion?"

Then, before Townsend could answer, Blatchford said, "I bet you mean Rad Devlin."

"Who's he?" asked Townsend.

"He's the rider that rode along in with you so

you wouldn't get lost," said Blatchford carelessly. "He wears his six-gun low that way because he's got boils."

Why sure, naturally, of course, thought Townsend.

"If you think I'm bringing in hired gunmen, you're crazy," said Blatchford good humoredly.

"How long he been with you?" asked Townsend.

"Not long," said Blatchford. "He rode in the other day hungry, and I fed him, and what with one thing and another, hired him."

An iron wagon rim hung suspended from an arm before the cookhouse. A man in an apron came out and began to beat it. "Supper," said Blatchford, getting up and starting for the ranch house door.

"Well, I'm hungry myself," said Townsend. Every ranch, of course, fed every visitor—drifter or cattle baron.

"Just go down to the cookhouse," said Blatchford. "And tell the boys I sent you personal. Be sure to mention that, and you'll get a joyous welcome. I can feed you, but I'm sorry I can't hire you."

There was, alongside the cookhouse, built into its side, a low stubby annex; the cookhouse was of logs but this building was of rough-sawed four-by-twelve planking. There was a table in it and through the open door Townsend could see the hands at the table, eating. Eating and busily, before the last vibration of the wagon rim gong had died down. That was what the ringing had meant: come and get it, and woe be to the cook that didn't have it there, waiting, ready to get. Townsend strolled in, took an empty place without plate or tableware, at the near end of the table, far spaced from the others clustered at the other end, said, "Passing through," and sat down.

They looked at him, and nodded. They looked hostile, but nodded. You'd nod to your worst enemy if he was guest at your table.

He saw no reason why he should fawn, so he returned their gaze just as coldly, and a little more so for good measure.

One by one, down one side of the table, around its end, and up the other side, he gave them an inspection, as though he were counting a handful of small change. And they didn't like it.

He was pretty sure that all of them, with the exception of two, this Rad Devlin who had brought him in and one other, a sullen looking character, milky-eyed and big-knuckled, were just harmless average ranch hands. These two tried to lock eyes with him but didn't get very far; Townsend had locked eyes with Yaquis.

Now one of them spoke, a stocky middle-sized man with crinkled jowls and a nice moderate voice. He said, "You better move down and join us. You cain't reach the food up there. Four feet from this crowd and you'll starve to death."

"Thanks," said Townsend and moved down. "Mark Townsend."

"Dave Prentiss," said the other. "Foreman here."

Now, before Townsend, there was food. Pot roast and brown gravy, onions and potatoes, sour dough biscuits and a bowl of molasses for the biscuits, or coffee or for just molasses, if that was the way your craving so ran. There was a huge bowl of pudding, raisin and rice, and a pot of coffee that smelled deliciously like burning tar paper.

The cook, red-faced, greasy, and sweating, came in from the door adjoining the cookhouse, skidded before him a chipped gray enamel plate, spoon, fork, knife, iron, bone-handled, coffee cup, no saucer, sighed in self-pity, and vanished. Townsend got to work.

There was a fiery discussion going on farther down the table and seemed to be getting a little tangled.

One cowboy said, "A thumb is not a finger. I don't care what your mamma and daddy told you when you was a boy. Pass the meat."

"If you want the meat, reach it yourself," said a second cowboy. "You ain't paralyzed."

The pallid man with the crinkled jowls and big knuckles said quietly, "Pass me the meat, Waddy."

Three hands came out quickly to oblige him. *He's a gunman, all right,* decided Townsend. The very way he acts, the way he sits among them and yet sits alone. He's a gunman and a stranger to them.

The conversation went back to thumbs. The second cowboy said, "My mamma and daddy said so. Are you calling them liars? And old folks knows."

"I ain't denying old folks knows," said the first cowboy. "I'm just gainsaying they ever said it. Let's consider a man's toes. He has ten of them, hain't he. And one on each foot is big, so it's called a big toe. If a man's thumb was actual a finger, why hain't it just called a big finger!"

The second cowboy screwed up his freckled face, pondered a minute, and then came in at an angle. "How many fingers has a raccoon got on each paw?"

"I've always counted five," said the first cowboy.

"But one's a thumb, ain't it?"

"Nacherally."

"There, you admit it."

"A racoon ain't a man. He cain't talk, for one thing. And his ears is considerable different, to say nothing of his tail. Anseer that!"

The friendly, intelligent-looking foreman, Dave Prentiss, said, "You finished, Mr. Townsend?"

Townsend said, "Yes, thank you. And it sure sits well."

"Then how about stepping outside and having a cigarette with me?"

"I'd appreciate it," said Townsend.

They left the table, the discussion over thumbs still raging, went outside, selected a patch of bare ground before the cookhouse, and sat down. They rolled cigarettes and got them going.

The foreman said, "Passing through."

"That's right," said Townsend. "Passing through."

"You know something," said Prentiss. "You scare me. And I've been here and there in my day and don't happen to spook at everything a breeze turns over."

"Scare you?" said Townsend, surprised. "Why?"

"I can't put it into words," said Prentiss, smiling.

"You didn't seem too scared over those two really mean characters, that Rad Devlin and his pal."

"That's right. Because Mr. Blatchford pays them, as he pays me, and I know whose side they're on."

Townsend said, "If I should tell you, honest, why I'm passing through, would you give me an honest answer to just one question?"

"I wouldn't much care to bind myself in such a proposition, but let's take a chance."

"Have you seen a pair of broke-down Apache

moccasins anywhere around? They have turned up toes and I think you would have noticed 'em. They was made for me by my Apache grandmother, adopted, and took from me at gunpoint by a fool who thought they was curious."

Prentiss thought this over, deliberately and at some length. "Apache," he said. "I'm glad I didn't steal 'em. No, I hain't seen 'em, and that's your honest answer. Now tell me why you're at our table this evenin', eatin' our food. That's your part of the trade."

"Is the country expecting a range war?" asked Townsend.

"How do I know what anybody's expecting? Besides, you've had yore question."

"Does Alf Teague think the WB outfit has been taking his cows. Right up that run?"

"Whoa, there, friend."

"Does he?"

"I'm gettin' not to like you quite so much."

"Here's why I'm here," said Townsend. "I'm getting ready to answer you, and, believe it or not, perfectly honest, without no shenanigans. A man named Joe Teague, Alf's brother, asked me to track a fellow, and paid me more than sufficient to do it, from the other side of the ridge. And started out to come along while I did it. Then this Joe Teague was shot down, no-show, by the man who took my moccasins and another, with me just sitting there, not lifting a hand. I decided to keep the pay, and decided to earn it."

"Do you think you'll ever find this man you was supposed to track?"

"See? You're doing the same thing—extra questions. I've already found him. Now, you're really tantalized, aren't you?"

"Yes."

"He's called Red River. He's a big Texan with fuzzy red fur. Starting tomorrow, he'll be the new foreman at Lazy M."

"They've already got a foreman, if you can call him that," said Prentiss. "Name of John Wilson."

"I've been told poor John Wilson fell off his horse down the trail a distance and kilt himself."

"Is that so?" said Prentiss, now boring his eyes into Townsend. "For a stranger just passing through, you seem even to be better informed than some of us locals."

Townsend grinned, arose, and asked, "How do I get to the Lazy M back pasture? The one they call Spruce Pasture."

"You don't get to it," said Prentiss, just vaguely evasive in his manner all at once, "unless you're a Lazy M man, or a Lazy M cow."

"What if I should get lost and stumble into it?"

"Well, chances are you wouldn't stumble out. Alf Teague lives in hysterics now that he's missing so many from his front pasture, and keeps Spruce pretty carefully watched."

"So long," said Townsend, and started for

the ranch house and his mare. He wasn't too comfortable. Somewhere along the line in the conversation things had changed. Things around him, ranch house, cookhouse, bunkhouse, stables and corrals, looked the same. But they didn't feel the same. Maybe he was seeing the two gunmen at the WB table. Maybe it was the note of deception, apparently unprovoked, that he had suddenly sensed in Prentiss. But the WB spread didn't give off that good old run-of-the-mill atmosphere to him the same way.

He turned north in a big semicircle, to cut into Spruce Pasture from the rear, from the mountains.

One thing he was sure of—there was range trouble brewing, all right.

VII

Crags and spruce, brush and outcrop and more spruce, that was what it was coming down the slope toward Spruce Pasture from behind. And rarely did Townsend get a view of the little valley below him, because of obstructions close to him, and when he was able to see it at all it was only a brief glimpse of rich buffalo grass and scattered cattle. If a man had especially fine cattle, this was the place to graze them all right, and keep an eye on them, too, to boot, which Prentiss said was Alf Teague's habit. After a bit, Townsend came into a little shelflike glade with a wet weather spring, holding now scarcely a hatful of water.

He dismounted, drank, watered his mare. Very recently indeed, the ground about it had been disturbed by a horse and a man. One man, and one horse, and the hoofprints, to the best of his memory, were strangers to him. The man's boot-prints also.

The man had felt secure. There had been no attempt to conceal them.

Townsend found ashes of a last night's camp-fire, and then the small hole of a picket stake. The rider had not only spent the night, but he had come from the mountains, not as would have seemed natural—from the Lazy M ranch house, and the valley below.

Where he was bound for was anybody's guess, maybe the Lazy M, maybe even in a roundabout way to the WB, most likely to Martinsburg to slake a powerful thirst.

He was mildly surprised to edge his mount around a thicket of scrub to confront him face to face.

He was sitting before an efficient little fire, eating a grouse which he had skinned, drawn—its guts lay tangled by his boot toe—and roasted. He was unalarmed at the sight of Townsend, but he didn't invite him to get down and join him. Dusk was gathering fast now, and in the ruby light of the fire coals, Townsend saw a bloated figure, a complete stranger to him. Nearby was his horse, patiently standing, and bearing a brand that sort of looked like two arrows crisscrossed over a circle. The brand was strange to Townsend also.

"This land is off-limits to strangers," he said shortly.

"Off-limits, off-limits," said Townsend. "That's all a traveler hears around here. Is there any land on-limits to strangers?"

"I hear most public cemeteries is on-limits to strangers," said the man. "What do you want here?"

"I want to talk to a certain man," said Townsend. "And from the way they give me, I got a feeling you might be him. That would save me a trip clean into Lazy M bunkhouse. You bear his resemblance. His name is John Wilson, and he's the Lazy M foreman."

The resemblance of this man to the man Townsend killed on the mountain couldn't have been more different.

"You've hit the nail on the head," said the man with an artificial smile. "John Wilson, in person. What can I do for you?"

"I want a job," said Townsend.

Instead of asking, What kind of a job? as Townsend naturally had expected, the man asked, "Who sent you?"

"Nobody sent me," said Townsend. "I just want a job."

Now it came, and it was pure show. "What kind of a job?"

"Wolfer," said Townsend.

"So you're a wolfer," said the other.

"Anything's possible," said Townsend.

"Where's your wagon?" asked the bloated man suspiciously, as Teague had asked him. "I never seen a wolfer without his wagon. He lives from that wagon, jest as a sheepherder lives from his'n."

"Up in smoke," said Townsend. "Burnt to hell and gone. Indians!"

"Indians?" said the man, interested. "Renegade war party, hey?"

"Oh, no," said Townsend. *If you're going to*

lie, go all out at it. "These was just a couple of sweet little Piute boys, maybe ten years old, that I picked up and gave a lift to. Darn their busy little souls, they got hold of my pipe when I laid it for a minute on the wagon seat between us, and dumped its red-hot coals, unbeknownst to me, into the bag where I carried my greasy skillet rags."

It was a glory and ecstasy to watch the man's face.

"Well," he said in disgust. "Now that-there is a fearful story. I swear and declare it's one of the most turrible Indian outrages I ever heered tell of. And I've heered my share."

"Well, I'll be getting on," said Townsend.

"Back the way you come," warned the man. "Up, not down."

Townsend turned and followed his orders.

He decided he'd learned about enough.

Now he was getting somewhere. He wanted to talk again to Holgate. Second day after, he came back into Martinsburg.

It was about ten o'clock at night when he returned. He tended his mare and walked across Holgate's backyard to the back door. Holgate was in his kitchen reading an old newspaper through spectacles low on his nose when Townsend came in, and he smiled with pleasure at the sight of him. He made no comment about Townsend's trip, nor asked any questions about it.

"We may have a visitor," he said.

"Who?" asked Townsend. He hung his rifle on the buckhorns and went to the stove to see if there was any leftover supper. There was cold spareribs, and cold biscuits.

Holgate said, "A fellow I asked to drop around for a few nights for maybe a game of euchre. A young fellow named Willie Dodd I happened to pass in town. I thought you might like to meet him."

"What's he do?"

"Not any more than he has to. Sweeps the floor in a saloon."

Townsend munched cold spareribs and biscuits.

There was a knock on the door. The young man who came in wore cast-off clothes, too long in the sleeves and too short at the ankles. He was incredibly dirty.

"This is Mr. Townsend, a friend," said Holgate. "Mr. Willie Dodd."

Townsend, surveying him, wondering what was what, noticed his feet. And saw the moccasins. His moccasins. Down to the last stitch, down to the last split and breakthrough.

"Glad to meet you, Mr. Dodd," said Townsend heartily. "Yes, indeed. I was just observin' your shoes. I don't mean any insult but they seem to be coming apart. But I find them enjoyable to look at. May I ask where you got them?"

Young Mr. Dodd's eyes were blank and his

jaws were slack and Townsend suddenly realized he probably wasn't the brightest human who ever drew breath.

"Bobbie give them to me," said the youth. "A feller give them to him, and he kept them until he got tired looking at them, then give them to me. See? The toes turn up."

"Bobbie who?" asked Townsend. "Where could I find him?"

"Why, where he works," said the youth. "Out at Lazy M."

"That's Bobbie Ashburton," put in Holgate. "He's been a longtime hand there, and was closer'n a shadow to John Wilson, the foreman, the pore fellow that kilt hisself fallin' from his horse over the ridge a while back."

"Look at my moccasins," said Townsend.

He looked at them himself, and thought of Joe Teague wearing them.

The young man, too, looked at them.

"Why don't you buy a pair like these?" asked Townsend.

"I couldn't afford them," said the youth, shaking his head in admiration.

"Top grain hide," said Townsend. "And no splits or rips or breaks."

"Almost spankin' new," said the young man.

"I'll tell you what I'll do," said Townsend. "I'll swap you yours for mine."

The word swap completely altered the boy.

Greed and avarice came into his face. He said, "I hain't shore I care to part with them. What do you offer extra? What's to boot? I don't mean jackknives and fishhooks. I'm thinking more in the line of money."

Townsend began to get mad. He'd had a long, mean trip. For an instant, he felt his control slipping.

Hurriedly, Holgate said, "Mr. Townsend comes from 'way yonder down south, Willie. Down there they swap different than we do up here. They don't make a strawberry festival out of the operation and spend the whole day at it. They get their swaps over as quick as you could snap your fingers. They don't start high and quibble down. They name their one and only price first off, and that's it. So this is final, Willie. Do you want them new moccasins of Mr. Townsend's, or don't you?"

"I want them," said the young man docilely.

Townsend exchanged moccasins with him.

The feel of his old friends on his feet again was like a dream.

The youth said, "Shall we get on with that euchre game, Mr. Holgate?"

"Let's skip it for tonight, son," said Holgate. "I seem to have what my grandma used to call a sick headache comin' over me."

"Goodnight all," said the youth as he left. "I'm afraid I out-traded you, Mr. Townsend. But that's the way it goes sometimes, ain't it?"

"That's the way it goes," agreed Townsend.

When the young man had left, Holgate said, "What were you thinking about there for a second?"

"Nothing," said Townsend.

"That's what I figured," said Holgate. "That's when the danger comes. When a man jest can't take no more and his mind goes sort of blank, and all he's thinking about is nothing. Feel better now?"

"Better," said Townsend, and smiled.

He got down two big china mugs from a shelf, filled them with coal black coffee from a chipped blue enamel pot at the back of the stove, and brought them to the table. He and Holgate sat down.

Now, watching Holgate's eyes as he talked, Townsend told him of his trip, as fully as possible, being careful to keep his conclusions and all personal opinion out of it.

"I know that line of cottonwoods, and that bluff, and passage up to the WB outfit from Lazy M you're speaking of," said Holgate. "And it's that passage, you might say, that's caused all the bad friendship between them. At first Alf Teague just hinted, and now he's just about coming out and saying that many a Lazy M front pasture cow has passed that bluff going north, maybe to eat WB grass."

Townsend said, "Has anybody ever seen anything?"

"No. But they've sure as hell tried."

"And yet there's going to be a range war over it?"

"Never say 'range war,' son," remarked Holgate. "The quickest way to get yourself a range war is just to keep saying it."

Townsend took a long drink of the black coffee.

"But," said Holgate.

"But what?"

"But I wouldn't want to be the man that went around blackguardin' Bill Blatchford. He's old-timey, and don't take to insults and such."

"I would think twice, myself," said Townsend. "And Alf Teague don't look like a reckless man to me."

"When somebody takes one of his cows, somebody takes two ten-dollar banknotes out of the wallet in his back pocket. And a thing like that can bear down on you."

Now Holgate took a long drink of coffee, down to the eggshell and grounds dregs.

Belching slightly, he said, "Which brings us to the rider you saw eating his grouse on the mountainside down by Spruce Pasture."

"The pasture no one ever gets into and no cow has ever been taken from," said Townsend.

"Up to now, let's say," answered Holgate. "The pasture, they tell us, with the best cows."

"The horse brand I mentioned," said Townsend. "The circle with the two crossed arrows. Is that another neighbor of Alf Teague's?"

"No," said Holgate slowly. "It ain't. I know it, but I doubt if they's too many others here in Martinsburg that does. It's the Circle X, from just out of Missoula, Montana. Ponder that over a minute, and tell me what you come up with."

"I can't make any sense out of it at all."

"Across the Flathead River, two hundred miles away."

"Well, one thing's certain," said Townsend. "Mr. Alf Teague better double his guard on that back pasture. Times mighty well could be fixing to change out at Lazy M. Could be they're getting interested in that back pasture, too, now."

Holgate yawned.

Townsend asked, "How did you come to know of this Circle X?"

"I used to live below the Flathead. It's well knowed down there. It has a good reputation."

"A good reputation is like a bad reputation. Easy to come by. But harder to swallow."

"Don't tell me you're fixing to pay a visit to the Circle X."

"It could be I wouldn't have to. Just another visit to the Lazy M, and a talk with our Bobbie Ashburton, the gentleman that collects other fellow's shoes."

"It's now Saturday night," said Holgate.

"Maybe you won't have to ride out to Lazy M. Maybe you can find him in town, at the Tip Top Saloon."

"I'm a tracker, but not a saloon-tracker, generally speaking. How do I find it?"

"They's two ways," said Holgate. "You can go in town and buy a drink somewhere, anywheres, and then another, and get drunk, and it will find you, because it's at the end of that line. Or you can go directly to it. It's in Artillery Alley."

VIII

The first man on Main Street Townsend asked about Artillery Alley simply gave him a grin, half knowing, half warning, and pointed.

It turned out to be a crooked dogleg passage extending back from Main Street itself, between a warehouse and a three-story brick office building. Townsend went down it about twenty yards, where it seemed to come to a dead end, but actually made an L-turn to the left. At the corner of the turn was a building of unpainted lumber and sagging windowsills that had been originally erected as a house. A vertical sign lighted by a coal oil lamp with a corrugated tin reflector, hung from the corner edge: *Tip Top.* Green window blinds tacked to the inside of the windows showed splinters of golden light at their rims.

There were two doors. The near one, and the one around the corner.

Townsend took the far door, the one around the corner, as this one would enter a different world, a far more private world than the nearer one, the more public one.

He found himself in a real rat nest. In fact, he had rarely seen worse.

The walls were simply lumber, ceiling and floor

the same. There were no decorations whatever, pictures or curtains, for these customers had no eye for decor. This place was indeed, as Holgate had declared, the end of the line. There were tables, round topped with peeling surfaces, and cheap wire-backed ice cream parlor chairs. The men at the tables, most tables with quarts on them, were a hodge-podge lot, all of them murderous looking. They were laughing, sleeping, talking, arguing. But the overall sound waves were not noisy. Get noisy in here, Townsend was sure, and out you went on your ear. Murderous, you could be confined within these walls and be properly handled. Noisy, and you were heard outside. And become a public nuisance and the town might object and step in.

Townsend sat down at an empty table just inside the door. When a waiter came to him, he ordered a quart and a waterglass. He knew he looked stone sober, and added the waterglass touch to put the waiter at ease. It did. He disappeared, returned with a murky looking quart, swept up a used, dirty waterglass from an adjacent table, and placed them before Townsend.

Townsend paid the waiter and he left.

Townsend poured a drink, carefully left it untouched, leaned back, and looked things over.

He saw Bobbie instantly, and with him, almost too good to be true, was his pal, the rifleman who had shot Joe Teague from his saddle, no-show, and finished him off on the ground so cold-bloodedly.

They were seated across the room, apparently as sober as he was. They saw Townsend too, but made a great show of not seeing him, and certainly not recognizing him if they had seen him.

They got to their feet. They looked exactly as they had when he had last seen them, like sorry chuckline cowboys with well-kept weapons—Bobbie in shabby, faded blues, his puckered-faced friend in cheap gingham shirt, and shapeless army-blue pants tucked into his boot tops. On their feet, they faced each other, talking gravely for a moment, then raised their hands in a half gesture of parting, and separated.

Which presented a problem to Townsend. But, after all, it was the pink cheeked Bobbie he wanted a session with.

There were three doors here. One to the front room, one to a closet or storeroom, probably, and the one by Townsend's right hand, the one through which he had just entered.

Bobbie started weaving his way through the tables toward this third door, directly toward Townsend.

This was as good as anything, so Townsend simply waited.

He passed Townsend by, however, eyes fixedly ahead, and exited through the nearby door, out into the open.

Townsend waited an instant to give him a little headway, and got up and followed.

Outside, he saw him. He hadn't turned the corner for Main Street, but was walking the other way, deeper into the alley.

The alley was black, but the moon was coming out from behind a veil of cloud fragments. Ashburton was scarcely twenty yards ahead. Townsend took out his six-gun as he walked, held it laxly at his knee, and quickened his pace.

He made no attempt at walking softly. He only hoped that Ashburton would hear him, and turn, and try to do something about it.

But the Lazy M hand was seemingly so unsuspecting that he did just about the opposite. He paused, lighted a cigarette, blew out the lucifer, and, all in the most apparent innocence, tossed the match aside and continued his stroll.

And then Townsend knew for a fact what he had decided before.

The man in front of him was a decoy. Townsend's real risk lay behind him.

It must have been a shock when they had seen him in the Tip Top. They knew he could be there under two conditions only: by sheer unbelievable chance, or because he was looking for them. If he was looking for them, this could only mean peril to them of the worst kind.

Shrewdly, they had decided to put it to a test.

What would he do now? Would he follow one of them?

Bobbie Ashburton had been selected as the bait. The other one, the one in the baggy pants, the man who had shot down Joe Teague, had been appointed the one to close in from behind. He had proved himself too much interested and was to be shot in the back, without the ghost of a chance of defending himself.

He had to be gotten out of the way.

He came to a carpenter shop built flush to the alleyway. It was deserted now for the night and black shadow hung over it. He stepped into its shallow doorway and waited.

He didn't have to wait long.

Almost instantly, he heard the footsteps. The awkward footsteps of a walking man trying to conceal the sound of his tread, a man who simply didn't know how.

The second one, the man in the baggy pants, came up from behind him. He was walking quickly, but half tiptoe, like a child. He had his Colt out, and half aimed before him, at full cock.

Townsend stepped out, rammed his six-gun low and up into the man's chest, so that the devastating blast would be as instantly fatal as possible, and shot him.

The man didn't even have time to show surprise.

Up the alley, Bobbie Ashburton heard the gun

roar, wheeled, and came running. He thought it was all over. He thought Townsend was in the dust, as dead as Joe Teague had been.

Townsend used the crook of his left elbow as a gun rest, waited until he was satisfied with the range of the man rushing toward him, and shot him three times. Bobbie Ashburton ran dead a half step and collapsed.

This wasn't the way Townsend had wanted it. He wanted the man alive, to answer questions. But other people could answer those questions. Red River, for instance.

He went into the carpenter shop's rear yard, found a division between two buildings, and eventually found himself again on Main Street.

Back in Holgate's kitchen, he could hear Holgate asleep in his long underwear, snoring softly in the dark. He undressed, and stretched out on his buffalo hide.

Perhaps an hour later there was a hammering at the door. They got up. Holgate lighted a lamp. Their visitor pushed in. It was Sheriff Purdy, now brisk. He faced Townsend.

"Ed Cushing and Bobbie Ashburton, Lazy M men, has been murdered," announced Sheriff Purdy.

So that was the name of the man in baggy pants, *Ed Cushing.*

Townsend turned to Holgate. "I never seen such a place for gunfights."

"This wasn't no gunfight," said the sheriff. "Cushing had his gun out, all right. But he was shot from the side, up through the chest. That wouldn't happen in a gunfight, it would be face to face. Bobbie Ashburton didn't even have his gun out, he jest lay there, shot three times."

"Why talk to me about it?" asked Townsend.

"I want to know if you did it."

"Do you think that would be my style?"

"Frankly, yes. I think if you wanted a man deal, you'd want him dead."

Townsend looked blank.

"I never cared for either of 'em," said the sheriff. "But that's beside the point. I understand you jest come in from a trip out to Bill Blatchford's WB."

He really keeps himself well posted, Townsend decided.

"You don't quite fit into this Idaho country somehow," said the sheriff. "It's hard to put into words, but you jest don't. Did Bill Blatchford bring you in to kill Lazy M men?"

"No," said Townsend, genuinely angry. "I wouldn't touch that kind of pay."

"Well, anyways," said the sheriff grimly, after a pause, "we've finally got it."

"Got what?" asked Townsend.

"The range war folks has been dreadin'. Alf Teague, all hair-triggered for trouble himself, and loathin' and abominatin' Blatchford, is going to lay it on WB."

When they were alone, Holgate said impassively, "Tell me all about it."

Townsend told him.

"Two of 'em, one, two," said Holgate. "Just like swattin' flies. And if it had been four, I'd bet it would have been the same. You'd have worked it out some way. Dave Prentiss was right, you are a spook. And Sheriff Purdy was right when he told you he figured you a desperate character. Even now it don't bother you. Not one bit."

"Don't talk that way," said Townsend, offended. "I'm no different from anybody, from you."

"Yo're what I might have dreamt to be once when I was a heap younger," said Holgate. "But fell mighty far short of."

Uncomfortable, Townsend changed the subject. "I've been to WB," he said. "It's hemmed in, all except that pass to Teague's front pasture, by impassable mountains. Say Blatchford *was* taking Lazy M cows, how would he get them out?"

"No mountains is impassable," said Holgate. "And you should know that. You could do like the Indians did, and rustlers do now, go around them at their feet. They's always ways. It's longer, but it'll get you there."

Townsend thought this over. "Yes," he said. "Yes."

And then he said, “And the same would be true of Teague’s Spruce Pasture, with all that choice stuff. So Circle X, down at Missoula, could find a way, if it had its eye set on them.”

“I’ve told you before,” said Holgate. “Circle X hain’t in the rustlin’ business.”

“One or more of its hands, then,” said Townsend. “Let’s put it that way. Every bunkhouse has its innocent looking thief.”

“Every bunkhouse,” agreed Holgate.

IX

Next morning, at an early breakfast, Holgate said, "Well, you got yore moccasins back."

"Right," said Townsend.

"And Bobbie Ashburton's passed on to his reward for this thoughtless mistake."

"Right."

"So yo're going to be sensible, and consider yore business here in Martinsburg finished, and be getting out?"

"Wrong," said Townsend. "And we've been over this before. I'm carrying Joe Teague's money. He was never give a chance. I'm going to try to look into the matter, and maybe straighten it out a little."

"Why?"

"Because, like I told you, I'm going to sure as hell keep the money. And I won't be beholden for orphan money to no one, even a dead man like Joe Teague."

"That might be the hardest money you ever earned."

"I doubt that. Fighting Yaquis was the hardest money I ever earned."

"Who's the oldest of us?" asked Holgate. "You or me?"

"You," said Townsend warily, suspicious of what was coming.

"If I was to give you some advice, what would you do?"

"I'd give it serious thought," said Townsend sincerely. "But I can't promise no more than that."

"Good enough," nodded Holgate. "Now let's see, how shall I put it? I'll put it this way. Say you was riding through some brush and smacked into a hornet's nest. It was jest there, peaceful and quiet, until you hit it, and half busted it. Then it went crazy. You wouldn't take off your hat and pound it some more, and try to whip it down until it was peaceful and quiet again, would you?"

"I'd get the hell out, but I'm not getting the hell out of here."

"I'm not asking you to. I'm jest suggesting for you to retire for a while."

When Townsend thought this over, Holgate said, "Just ponder it a minute. Here's a peaceful valley with nothing happening but a little not-too-important rustling of Lazy M cattle going on. Then words start between Lazy M and WB. Words can happen anywhere but Bill Blatchford don't care for 'em and hires a couple of professional gunmen, because I'm sure Devlin and his pal are professionals, brought in for that purpose, to stand up agin Alf Teague, and for that purpose alone."

"I'm beginning to agree," said Townsend.

"And then what do you do?" asked Holgate.

"Well, first, back on the trail, you take Lazy M's foreman, John Wilson, away from them. We will not go into the whys, hows, and wherefores. But he shows up missing at the ranch, don't he? Then what? Then, after a bit, the same unhappy vacancy has happened to Bobbie Ashburton and Ed Cushing. Ed Cushing is going to be missed especially, he was their part-time blacksmith."

Townsend simply sat and listened.

"That's going to be a sort of empty bunkhouse at Lazy M," said Holgate. "I hope the rest, Mark Townsend's spares, can play mouth harps or something."

"There's plenty of other cowhands available," said Townsend. "Not like them, maybe, but others."

"Oh, it won't be empty long," said Holgate. "It'll be filled. But not with cowhands, with fellows who are half-cow hands, half gun-hands. You see what you've did, don't you? In trying to do this Joe Teague a favor, you've did a fellow you hadn't never heard of, Bill Blatchford, a disfavor. Somebody, either him or Alf Teague, is going to get plugged in person before it's over."

"I didn't start it," said Townsend. "It was started before I ever took the job."

"I know," said Holgate, genuinely apologetic. "I spoke in anger. My elements got the best of me. Now here's what I want you to do. I want you to stay right here as my guest, doin' nothing.

Absolutely nothing. Until you see what happens after last night in the alley by the Tip Top. Will you do that?"

"Yes," said Townsend. "On one condition?"

"I ain't sure I'm going to like one of Mark Townsend's conditions. What is it?"

"That I take one more trip out to Lazy M. I've got to talk to Alf Teague again."

"That's out of the question. You wouldn't come back alive. It would be impossible right at this very instant. Even yore best friends in them valleys would shoot just about anybody down at the drop of a hat."

"I don't have any best friends in those valleys."

"If a man had two ways of doin' a thing," said Holgate. "An easy way, and a hard way in which he'd be a certain loser, which should he take?"

Townsend waited, wooden faced.

Holgate said, "Talk to Alf Teague, here in town. Alone, o' course, but in some public place with no gunmen in sight, his or Bill Blatchford's. How does that sound?"

"Where would that be and how would it be managed?"

"I'd say on that green wagon seat bench on the sidewalk in front of Merriman's Feed & Grain."

"That would be all right, but how would we do it?"

"Bobbie Ashburton and Ed Cushing must be at the undertaker's right now. You can be sure a fast rider started to Lazy M to take the news as soon as their demise was official. If I know Alf Teague, he'll come in like an arrow to learn all about it, maybe riding night and day. This is Sunday. We'll make the date for about suppertime Tuesday."

"But how?"

"We'll send Willie Dodd, the card player you got back your moccasins from last night, to ride out and meet him, wherever that might turn out to be. Willie would do anything for a silver dollar."

"And what would Willie tell him?"

"That's part of it. Keep it secret sounding so it will interest him. Just say a certain man who seen his brother Joe killed has information for him much to his advantage and will talk to him at that time, alone, on that bench."

"All right," agreed Townsend. "We'll try it."

For the next couple of days, to Holgate's stern insistence, Townsend lay about the house, wound tight as a spring, doing nothing, keeping out of public gaze.

From Sunday until Tuesday, Townsend stayed so confined, in isolation behind Holgate's walls, but Holgate, shuttling to town and back thrice daily, kept in touch with things and brought the current news. And there was news, all right. A feeling had come over Martinsburg and the county, a sort of mixture between panic and blood-thirsty anticipation. There would be a range war, everyone said, there was no doubt about it. The question was when it would flame forth, and where.

About five on Tuesday afternoon, for Martinsburg ate early suppers, Townsend got ready for his excursion into town. Holgate suggested he accompany him, but Townsend left. "He's slippery and quick tempered, and that can be a bad combination."

"I want to get this over with," said Townsend.

Merriman's Feed & Grain was on the other side of Main Street, the less respectable side, beyond the little boxlike railroad station which stood like an island in the center of the broad road. Townsend had a good view of its front as he crossed the street toward it, and realized that Holgate had selected it as a meeting place because of this, so he wouldn't walk into anything blindly.

He saw the green wagon seat bench and its two seated occupants, for there were two. One was Alf Teague. In spite of the message sent to him to come alone he had brought along a companion.

The companion, Townsend saw as he came up, was Red River, the big red-haired Texan. Each of the two was powdered with dust from hard riding, and each of them looked at him blankly, not suspecting that he could possibly be their man.

This was the hottest hour of the day. The air was still and scorching and the sun, low in the west, was like a steel disc just taken from a forge.

Townsend was annoyed that Teague had violated the plan and brought his new foreman, but otherwise the situation bothered him not at all. He had only scorn for men like Red River.

He said, “Mr. Teague, I’m Mark Townsend, remember? The man you had this appointment with. I see you brought along a house pet.”

“The wolfer,” said Teague, hiding his astonishment.

“You mean the tracker,” said Red River in an ugly rasp. “The weasel that followed me across the ridge.”

“I’m on business now,” said Townsend. “But I wouldn’t be surprised if the two of us didn’t have a little talk about that weasel sometime later.”

“Well, if you’ve got business,” said Teague curtly. “Get on with it.”

“I will,” said Townsend. “And not for your sake, for my sake. I’ve got some of your brother’s money I want to earn and get out. I think you’ve been looking at him completely backwards, or at least such could be possible. I think he was a true brother to you, maybe even truer than most. I think that ’way down there in Colorado he learned how them front pasture cows of yours were being stole up here. I think he dropped everything and came north up here to warn you about it.”

“Then why was he trackin’ me?” asked Red River.

Townsend, ignoring him, said to Teague, “Now that it’s coming out into the open, I doubt if another will ever be stole.”

“How was it being did?” asked Teague, contemptuously.

“I think certain of your own hands were in cahoots together and were taking them.”

There was a moment of silence.

When Teague was ready to speak, he said, “You mean, for instance, the late John Wilson?”

“Could be.”

“And Robbie Ashburton and Ed Cushing?”

“I’d say yes.”

“You think, you think, you think,” said Teague, now flushed-cheeked. “You know what I think?”

“I don’t much care,” said Townsend. “I’ve done my job.”

“I think you’re repeating words you’ve been told to say. I think you’re working for Bill Blatchford. You was seen going onto his place not long back.”

“Shall I dust him around a little, boss?” asked Red River.

“Forget him,” said Teague. “The day of judgement is coming, and soon. He’ll get his then, along with the others.”

They got up and left.

Townsend watched their backs as they crossed the road.

He was about to turn away himself when a man, a stranger, walked up to him and said, "Can you spare a moment? Let's sit down and take a load off our feet."

Townsend hesitated, and they sat side by side on the wagon seat.

The man wore steel-rimmed spectacles and had a jolly face. He wore a long loose jacket of corduroy, coffee colored, and tan canvas pants. He looked like a prosperous stockman. Almost. Somehow, though, he was a bit too immaculate for a working stockman. A stockman would have had baggy pockets in that jacket, filled with just about everything. And there would have been at least one stain of some kind on his pants.

"Hot!" he said, wiping his throat with a new blue bandanna. "Whew!"

"Hot," said Townsend, playing along, feeling in his bones that this was going to develop into something, and wondering what.

The man said, "Hot or cold we're always complainin', hey? I'm Lucius Goodhue from the Buck Rock country."

Townsend nodded. He didn't offer his own name. He didn't believe the Goodhue part or the Buck Rock part either.

"Wasn't that Mr. Alf Teague I jest seen you talking to?"

"Yes," said Townsend.

"Work for him?" asked the man.

Now things were beginning to get interesting. Townsend decided to go whole hog. "Yes," he said. "He's a mighty good boss."

"What do you do, if I may so inquire?"

"Wolfer," said Townsend.

"Many such varmints out at Lazy M?" asked the man, to be sociable but totally uninterested in this particular point.

"They was," said Townsend. "They're getting scarcer."

They sat for a moment in silence, watching an enormous swarm of gnats hovering like vapor in the yellow sunset.

"Wolfer," said Goodhue thoughtfully. "A wolfer gets pretty well over a spread, don't he?"

"Inch by inch," said Townsend in mock weariness.

"Been all over that front pasture, I guess."

"Oh, yes."

"The back pasture, too? Spruce Pasture?"

"Naturally."

"They say there's good cows in that back pasture," said Goodhue.

"We ain't supposed to discuss that back pasture," said Townsend kindly. " 'Never talk about Spruce Pasture to no one whatever,' says Mr. Teague."

"Mr. Teague wouldn't see no harm in it, not

with me," said Goodhue. "You see, I'm a cattle buyer, and I'm going to talk to him myself on the very subject. It just come to me that I'd like to have an outsider's opinion, too."

"Well, in that case, I'll tell you," said Townsend. "They're the finest. The finest you ever saw. I only wish I owned a dozen, any dozen."

"Then I hain't made my trip for nothing," said the man, and he couldn't keep a heavy double meaning from coming out in the tones of his voice.

He got up and held out his hand. In its open palm was a half dollar. "Have a drink on me," he said jovially.

Townsend let it lay, and stepped slightly back. "I was brought up never to touch spiritous liquors," he said in stiff reproach. "And, for that matter, never to associate with anybody that did!"

"No harm meant," said Mr. Goodhue hastily, pocketing the coin. And then, with a sudden touch of sarcasm coming into his voice, he added, "You must lead a pretty lonesome life."

"Yes," said Townsend. "When you come right down to it, I do."

He walked away.

Main Street at this hour, suppertime, was almost deserted, but Sheriff Purdy stood in the doorway of the apothecary shop, munching a vile looking gummy licorice stick. He offered one to

Townsend as he approached and Townsend shook his head. Townsend came to a stop. He said, "I don't know what's come over me, but I was about to look you up."

"I never thought I'd see that day," said the sheriff. "What's on your mind?"

Townsend described the man he had just been talking with, and passed on, almost word for word, the conversation. "I thought you ought to know," he finished. "I'm pretty sure he's no cattle buyer, and I doubt greatly if his name is Goodhue or that he comes from any Buck Rock country."

"He's a cattle buyer, his name is Goodhue, and he comes from the Buck Rock country," said the sheriff. "I've rode across his land many and many a time. It's about forty mile east o' here."

"Well, I don't like him," said Townsend.

"Maybe he didn't like you either," said the sheriff mildly. "But jest didn't show it because he was too busy pumping you."

"Do you like him?" countered Townsend.

"I ain't supposed to answer yes or no to a question like that," said the sheriff. "But I'll tell you one thing. I got an old yaller hound dog I like better."

Townsend grinned. "I just wanted to tell you this," he said. "Watch him."

"I find that important and surprising coming from you," said Sheriff Purdy. "Because I'm so busy watching you. But I'll do it, son."

They stood there for a minute, enjoying each other wordlessly.

Finally, the sheriff said, “It’s suppertime. My stomach has drawed itself up to the size of a pool ball. I’ll stand treat for a meal somewhere.”

“I’d like to,” said Townsend genuinely. “But Mr. Holgate has already mixed up a extra big bowl of that specialty of his—eggs, onions, green peppers, and chopped ham, for an omelet, and if I don’t show up, his foal won’t eat it.”

“I always heard it would eat anything,” said the sheriff in disbelief. “Even the cigars out of a man’s breast pocket.”

“Cigars, yes,” said Townsend. “Green peppers, no.”

They lifted their right hands slightly in farewell, at the wrists, and parted.

Holgate’s cottage was far out on the fringes of town. In fact, it was so far out that it was only doubtfully within the limits of town at all. Between the cottage and the thickening of buildings which was Martinsburg’s real edge was a quarter mile of desolate waste, spotted here and there by a hut or shanty or shack, but mainly knots of clumped saplings, arid earth, and bushy hummocks of tall dead grass. The road to the valleys north, Lazy M and WB and a few others, much smaller, wove its way through this sterility. Townsend had traversed it about halfway when he came to the campfire.

The campfire with skillet and potatoes and bacon in the skillet, with the three men sitting cross-legged about the embers, smoking brown paper cigarettes, waiting for the food to cook, three horses picketed, short picketed, beyond the firelight. The entire group seemed held in by the little ball of pink glow, the firelight in the dusk.

There were two things mighty apparent to Townsend as he approached. They were a hard traveled trio, and a tough trio. Two of them wore Levi's and cotton shirts, once checked but now grimy beyond coloration. The third, scarred batwing chaps and a whipcord blouse. Their guns were tied low, and the man in the chaps wore two of them.

Their faces and necks were dust-seamed in creases. They had ridden hard and fast, all right. You rode that way sometimes to get away from somewhere, but you rode that way sometimes, too, to get somewhere—if you were needed.

The short picket on their horses told Townsend they wouldn't be here long. They were going to throw down some food and get on.

As Townsend came abreast of them, the one in the chaps, obviously their leader, said, "This one will do as good as any." To Townsend, he said coldly, "Come over here."

Leisurely, Townsend walked over.

One of the two in Levi's, lantern-jawed, slot-eyed, wicked looking, said, “And who are you?”

The other in Levi’s said contemptuously, “Looks like someone throwed off a freight car.”

The man in chaps said, “What’s the closest way to Lazy M?”

Townsend told them, as a woodsman would, with great brevity and clarity. They listened like experts.

When he had finished, the man in the chaps said, “Anything especial holding you?”

“No,” said Townsend.

“Then dust,” said the man in the chaps. “Good-bye, adios, get gone.”

Townsend sauntered on.

Professional gunmen, if he’d ever seen any. Hired by Alf Teague, probably, the moment Bill Blatchford had brought in Devlin and his companion, just arriving.

This was the day of judgement Teague had spoken of.

And it had come.

X

Sitting at Holgate's kitchen table, supper just finished and the empty plates before him, Townsend said, "One thing I don't understand too clear. I'm thinking about the WB outfit. After the autumn roundup. How does it get its cows to the railroad for shipping? Through the notch and out across Alf Teague's front pasture?"

"No," said Holgate. "Teague won't allow him or his cattle on Lazy M land."

"Then how?"

"He gets 'em into town here the same way he and his hands gets in when they want to come. You know we was talking about no mountains being really impassable? Well, they's a back door, or side door really to the WB. Bill Blatchford's little valley is shaped like a long loaf of bread. At the south end, the end nearest Martinsburg and the railroad and the chutes, they's broad U-shaped gap. It's actually a shortcut for them, from their ranch house, that is. The line runs straight as a ramrod down their prairie. Through the gap, to town." He got down the map he had previously drawn and added a new straight line. "See?"

Townsend said, "That's the way I'll take."

Holgate asked, "When?"

"Right now. Right this very minute. If I hurry, I

might get to the WB bunkhouse before dawn."

"Oh, you can do it, all right," said Holgate reprovingly. "It's not only a shortcut, but once you get through the gap it's easy going, plains and prairie grass. Just keep riding straight at the Big Dipper. But don't you remember we come to an agreement you was to give this thing a rest for a little while."

"You come to that agreement, not me, exactly."

"But yore all finished. You've as much as said so."

"I've changed my mind. People go around threatening me and I don't like to be threatened." He paused.

"I want to warn Dave Prentiss. He's the only man I've talked to, except you and Sheriff Purdy, that didn't act like I was loose from a cage."

"I've changed my mind. I think you are." Holgate looked solemn.

Townsend got up and took down his rifle.

Holgate said, "Want me to go along? You might fall off your mare and kill yourself, like that John Wilson feller did."

"I'll have to take that chance," said Townsend. "But thanks."

Holgate told him how to reach the gap.

The WB ranch buildings were silver and sooty black in the moonlight just before dawn, when Townsend tied his mare behind the stable and took a position in shadow a little closer, where he could watch the bunkhouse. A light showed at the rear of the cookhouse, which was as he expected for the cook would be the earliest riser. No light showed in the ranch house, none from any of the barns as yet, none from the bunkhouse. He relaxed and waited for the stirring, the ranch's gradual awakening.

After a bit, the bunkhouse door opened, an oblong of black in the now graying light, and a man emerged. A stunted man in his drawers; Rad Devlin, the one of Blatchford's pair of gunmen whom Townsend had really met, he decided. The man walked about ten feet, urinated, and went again inside.

Shortly after he was followed by a second man who went through the same procedure, and then another, and then another.

This, Townsend knew, this parade of sleepy urinators, took place without variation in every bunkhouse in the country, every morning without exception. Rain or shine; in rain they would come out in their oilskins and drawers.

Eventually, Dave Prentiss came out.

Townsend whistled softly. He stepped out and revealed himself, and Prentiss, who recognized him instantly, came forward to join him. Townsend said, "I've got a couple of interesting things to tell you. Let's get out of sight, and maybe sit down someplace."

There was a runway between two sheds, roofed

over at the top and floored with corncob litter and hay. They seated themselves just within its dark mouth where they could keep the little group of ranch buildings under a watchful eye. Prentiss, having no doubt that this was important, said nothing, not even a word of greeting.

Townsend said, “Know a man named Goodhue from the Buck Rock country? Fiery red jolly looking face, steel-rimmed spectacles?”

“Know of him. And have seen him a couple of times at roundups, sales, and such. Important stockman down in his country, they say. Buyer, seller, and does a little feeding. Why?”

“Could be he’s fixin’ to perform the miraculous. Could be he’s aiming to buy out Alf Teague’s Spruce Pasture herd.” Townsend told Prentiss about his talk with him, and about the sneaky way Goodhue had tried to pump him.

“Well,” said Prentiss thoughtfully. “Think of that.” He paused. “Very fascinatin’, but did you come clean out here in the dead o’ night jest to pass it on to me?”

“That, and two other things,” said Townsend. He then told him about the rider he had seen with the Circle X horse, at the campfire on the mountainside above Spruce Pasture. “He wasn’t a honest man,” said Townsend. “Not to my lights, and I give that word a good wide leeway. They was larceny bone-deep in him, you could almost smell it.”

"What do you think he was up to?" asked Prentiss.

"I think he was going to size up that Spruce Pasture herd, for purposes of his own."

There was a moment of silence, and Townsend chuckled.

"What's funny?" asked the WB foreman.

"I was just thinking," said Townsend. "I was just thinking what if he should steal the back pasture cows as Mr. Goodhue was all set to buy them."

"That don't sound funny to me," said Prentiss. "If one, just one, cow vanishes from that back pasture Alf Teague will think we done it, and foam at the mouth and have a sure enough tantrum. The fat will really be in the fire."

"The fat was in the fire," said Townsend, "when your boss brought in this Rad Devlin and that other gunman, the one with the big knuckles. All of which brings me to my third piece of information."

He told him about the three men who had inquired directions to Lazy M, the two in Levi's, and their leader in scarred chaps. "Hired killers, if I ever saw any," said Townsend. "Alf Teague's army has arrived. You better tell your boss *that*."

"I will," said Prentiss. "Maybe sometime I can do as much for you."

He got up and left. Townsend left, too.

It was four minutes after eleven that night when

Townsend came in Holgate's kitchen door and by twelve after he was on his buffalo hide, boots off but otherwise fully dressed, sound asleep. He had been awake almost forty hours, at least twenty-four of them on his mare, the last twelve without any food whatever. Holgate had looked him over casually for blood smears, seen none, had mixed him a coffee can of elderberry wine with a little ground cloves and cinnamon plus a couple of broken eggs, and pointed to the pallet in the corner. When Townsend had started to speak, Holgate said, "Tomorrow—we'll hear all about it tomorrow."

The next thing Townsend knew, Holgate was putting on his boots, there was morning sunlight through the open door, and the kitchen was filled with the smell and stuttering of frying bacon.

A week went by, and the first touch of autumn came. It came one night with a sudden steady rain, no thunder or lightning or threshing of wind, just a heavy sodden downfall. The yellow burned grass lay flat next morning. After the rain, the sky went crystal clear and dazzling blue, and two nights later came the thick frost, burning the mountain foliage to copper and crimson in icy fire. The air became spicy and fragrant, like the inside of a cider barrel.

Townsend, at Holgate's insistence, found himself staying on, and even, little by little, discussing his future with Holgate. “Why go back to Arizona?” persisted Holgate. “Idaho’s a new country, with a future. It needs people just like you.”

“I like Idaho,” said Townsend. “But what would I do? I’ve tried cattle, and failed.”

“You ain’t had a fair chance. You ain’t met up with the right people.”

“The right people?”

“That’s right. They’s men around here, too, old-timers mostly now, who have saw more blood spilled when they were young than they saw hot vegetable soup. Bill Blatchford, for one. Though you’d never guess it now. You met him, but you didn’t get to know him. You could be Bill Blatchford’s son.”

“His son?”

“His wayward son, let’s put it that way.”

Daily they expected to hear something from the county, a clash of some kind, barn burnings, or an ambush, but nothing happened. One day, Holgate, relaxing, said, “Maybe they’ve had their fun jest making turrible faces at each other and maybe, now that that’s been did, and nobody backed away, these outsiders will go back wherever they come from. It’s happened many a time that way before. Everybody has showed everybody that nobody is afraid of nobody.”

That Thursday at noonday dinner, Townsend said abruptly, “Tomorrow I move on.”

"Where to?" asked Holgate, only half concealing his disappointment.

"Arizona again, I guess," said Townsend.

"Suit yourself," said Holgate. "If yo're looking for Arizona, it's still there. If yo're looking for being twenty-one years old again, it ain't there no more."

"Be that as it may," said Townsend, "I've finished my job and earned my money and I'm moving on."

"Then tonight we'll have us a feast," said Holgate. "What would you like most of all to eat?"

"You haven't got the nerve to hear it," said Townsend.

"Did you say a thick steak? Well then that's exactly what we'll have, with hash browns. Do you think you'll be going into town this afternoon?"

"Why not? I'd be glad to."

"Then get a couple of good T-bones at Baughman's. As you probably remember seeing by now, it's on Main Street next door to McLennan's."

At first, late that afternoon when Townsend turned onto Main Street, the street seemed deserted, for housewives were fussing around supper fires all over town, and hungry husbands were already sitting at tables holding their knives and forks and making impatient conversation. Sunlight filtered in splinters from the long uneven marquee down to the boardwalk and passersby were few. At first. Then, as Townsend came closer to his shop, he saw more people. They were going into McLennan's Saloon. Something was being displayed there. He wondered what? Maybe a two headed calf, or maybe a handcuffed and ankle-ironed prisoner, passing through with some out-of-country marshals.

He decided to go in and take a look himself.

Inside, McLennan's was a big place with tasseled draperies and a chandelier and much mahogany, an imitation of an imitation of someone's fancy of a deluxe establishment in Frisco. Townsend had never been here before; Holgate had told him while the liquor was the same as elsewhere, the prices were triple.

There was a medium-large crowd inside. The tables had been pushed back, leaving an open space in the center of the floor, and the gawkers stood in a thin circle around this space. It was almost as though they were going to hold a square dance.

Almost, but not quite.

A dead man lay on the floor, stretched out, ankles together, hands straight down at his sides as though he were at attention on the flat of his back. You could tell this, and that he was stone dead, despite the fact that he was covered with a window drape, yellow, fringed, with tasseled corners, which had been carefully laid over him as though he were a precious statue.

Sheriff Purdy pushed briskly through the circle of gapers, bent over, and carefully turned back the covering.

The man was Dave Prentiss.

Townsend hardly recognized him at first, he had been so badly pistol-whipped.

"Yes," said Sheriff Purdy, in a voice of toneless rage. "Dave Prentiss. And if there was a better, more decent man, I never met him. Some of you gentlemen carry him to the undertaker's." Turning, he said, "Now let's hear that again."

The bartender, in apron and hat came forward. "We were just chatting, several of us at the bar, when we heard it from the alley out behind. Later, we counted as best we could the gunshots in him. As near as we could make it, they was close to twenty-four. That means that four fellers with six-guns just emptied their weapons into him."

"I can figger," said Sheriff Purdy curtly.

Or, thought Townsend, *two fellers in Levi's, with a six-gun each, and one fellow in chaps with two six-guns.*

"You said there was a note pinned to his shirtfront," said Sheriff Purdy. "I'd like to see it."

The bartender walked behind the bar and returned with it.

Sheriff Purdy read it, strolled across the open space past the dead man, and handed the note to Townsend.

It read: *In part payment for Bobbie Ashburton and Ed Cushing.*

To the barman, the sheriff said, “Told anybody about this yet?”

“No, sir.”

“Then don’t, understand?”

“Yes, sir.”

Someone in the crowd called, “What does it say, Sheriff?”

“Wait and find out,” said Sheriff Purdy, like the snap of a steel trap. To Townsend, he said, “Shall we go outside?”

Townsend nodded.

XI

They walked about ten feet down the walk, to where a sign read: *Baughman, Meats.* Townsend said, "I'll see you later. I've got to get a couple of steaks for our supper. Mr. Holgate wants something special for our supper. I'm leaving tomorrow."

"Get 'em," said the sheriff, coming to a halt. "I'll just wait here. I've got something to discuss with you."

Townsend entered the shop, was gone a few minutes, and returned with his package.

Before the waiting sheriff could speak, Townsend said, "I've got a question to ask you. Why, when you wouldn't show anyone else that note, did you show it to me?"

"I'll answer that in a minute," said Sheriff Purdy. "Let me see the palm of your right hand."

Townsend held out his arm and turned his hand over, palm up.

"Now raise it a little, so I can see it better," said Sheriff Purdy.

Townsend wondering what was up, did as requested.

"Now say 'I do,' " said the sheriff.

Townsend flinched, but said, "I do. Don't tell me that means you and me is now married?" Sheriff Purdy, not smiling, said quickly, "It means you're my new, and only, by the way, deputy. You've jest took the oath."

"I didn't hear any oath."

"I said it to myself, and that makes it more valid. That's why I let you read that note in there. Because you were the same as my deputy, even then."

"I don't want any part of it, Sheriff Purdy. I think you're all right, okay, but I don't want any part of it. I'm a wandering man."

"You'll still be a wandering man. Only difference is, I'll be telling you where to wander." In a low voice, he said, "Back me up, Mark. Back me up. I'm going to need somebody I can trust, somebody that knows about things, somebody that can do the job. This could be hell."

"And you picked me?"

"And I picked you."

"I never heard of a sheriff without any deputies before," said Townsend.

"Oh, I got a couple of fellers that calls themselves such. One is the mayor's son and the other is mighty good with a broom and dustpan, but I don't see them too often. You see they has an endless contest going on just between the pair of them down at the Acme Poolroom."

After an intense pause, Townsend said, "All right. I don't know anything at all about it, but I'll do it."

"Go home to Mr. Holgate's," said the sheriff.

"Eat and enjoy those farewell steaks for the farewell that ain't going to come off after all, and meet me at the courthouse in a couple of hours."

After supper at Holgate's, which each of them enjoyed immensely, despite the tragedy and new excitement, for they were men trained on hardship and had long ago learned to enjoy themselves whenever the rare opportunity offered itself, after the steaks and potatoes were gone and their plates were clean, Holgate said, "I hate to hear from you that Dave Prentiss has gone." He spoke as though the WB foreman had simply caught a train somewhere, and he missed him.

Townsend merely flattened his lips and said nothing.

"But I'd like to come back to the heart o' the matter," said Holgate. An atmosphere of great gravity came into the room as he spoke. "I'm referrin' to yore being chose by Sheriff Purdy as his new deputy, and what he told you on the side. Because he wanted a man like you to back him up in bad trouble. You cain't even begin to know the honor he's paid you. You've got to know Sheriff Purdy."

"I'll do my best," said Townsend humbly.

"Don't think he doesn't realize that. And don't think he doesn't realize how powerful your best can be. But what means a lot more to me is that he likes you. You know what I think?"

"What?"

"I think you'll be a law officer until you die, and that will be of old age. I think the time will come when yore name will be knowed on both sides of the Rockies."

"Then you think I got maybe what it takes?" asked Townsend, concerned.

"I think you got a heap more than it takes, and that's the trouble," said Holgate. "But you'll smooth out a little."

They sat there saying nothing. Then Holgate said, "Yes, sir, son. It's a gift of God. You've finally hit yore right groove."

"One thing more," said Townsend. "I'd like to live here with you."

"You're welcome and more than welcome," said Holgate delighted.

"I'll pay you room and board, of course," said Townsend.

"Would you pay yore father room and board?"

"Yes."

"Well, I ain't yore father. We'll talk about that later. Have another mug o' coffee?"

"The first big lesson in deputing," said Sheriff Purdy to Townsend a little later, as they sat in the sheriff's office at the courthouse, across the sheriff's desk from each other, "is never to let nobody never look you down nor away. But that's a weakness I have a feeling you hain't bothered with."

The sheriff's office had new plastered walls, the plaster so thin it almost looked like the laths had been covered with only a thick gritty whitewash, a floor of brown stained pine, a broken-down oilcloth sofa with a gleaming vicious looking spring sticking up from it, the desk and two chairs. Sheriff Purdy, you realized instantly, was a man who lived for his work and not for show.

"You can sleep here, on the couch," said the sheriff. "That busted spring ain't bad after you learn how to subdue it. You can get your meals at the Rosebud Cafe, and put it on the county bill, like I do. You'll work on a basic salary, which I'll go into later, plus fees for serving of papers, which also I'll go into later."

"I'm already fixed up room and board at Mr. Holgate's," said Townsend.

"That suits me," said the sheriff. "Now I've given you the first lesson in how to be a deputy. The second is that a deputy should never lie to his sheriff unless he so chooses, and if he so chooses then that automatically makes him a second-rate deputy. You understand?"

"Yes."

"All right. Now I want to ask you a question. Was it you who killed Bobbie Ashburton and Ed Cushing in the alley behind the Tip Top Saloon?"

"Yes, it was me. They had it in mind to do the same to me. I also killed John Wilson back over the ridge. Do you still want me?"

"You bet I do," said Sheriff Purdy. "Just simmer down, and tell me all about it."

Townsend told him about it. All about it. From the moment Joe Teague had darkened the sunlight, bending down coming through the door of his shack to hire him. He then told him the conclusions he and Holgate had come to about the whole affair.

He told him about the three gunmen just arrived at Lazy M.

The sheriff knew about this.

"They're the ones that killed Dave Prentiss and left that note," finished Townsend.

"I think so, too," said Sheriff Purdy. "But o' course I'm not a judge and jury, I'm jest a hit-and-miss wage earner."

The next four days, too, were uneventful. Townsend slept and ate at Holgate's, as before, and spent his time at the courthouse, and in serving papers, mainly, within a small radius of the town. He didn't care much for this sort of work but understood it was part of his job.

Once, at breakfast, Holgate said, "Did you ever stop and think about when the sheriff said you could sleep in the office and charge your meals at the Rosebud Cafe?"

"What about it?" asked Townsend, fork halfway to his mouth.

"Do you think for a minute that a deputy, or the sheriff himself for that matter, eats at the Rosebud and charges his meals to the county? The county pays fees and salaries, and nothing more. Yo're supposed to pay yore own living expenses. What would happen would be you'd charge it, and the sheriff would pay it—out of his own pocket."

"Why?" said Townsend, startled.

"Maybe because he likes you, maybe because he needs you."

After an interval, Townsend said, worried, "Be honest with me. Do you think I can do it?"

"Do what?"

"Straighten this county out."

Shocked, Holgate said, "Son, you ain't supposed to straighten this county out. You ain't supposed to straighten anything out. Yo're just supposed to help the sheriff. Do what he feels inclined to tell you. That, and nothing else."

"And if he don't tell me, do what I think he'd want me to do?"

"Now you got the idea."

Later that morning, about a quarter of eight, as Townsend was on his way to the courthouse to report for the day, he was passing down the walk on Main Street when he saw Mr. Goodhue. He was just getting out of the hotel rig at the station platform. He had a canvass valise in his hand, all set for traveling. The sun glinted on his steel-rimmed spectacles and his jolly face was more than jolly, actually radiant with happiness and satisfaction. *He's bought his cattle from*

Lazy M, all right, some of those Spruce Pasture cattle, the best, and at a good price, a more than satisfactory deal, Townsend decided. He sat down on an empty box before a store and waited.

Mr. Goodhue went into the station. A few minutes later a train puffed up to the station, steaming in bursts of vapor. Mr. Goodhue came out of the station and boarded it. The train pulled out.

Townsend got up, crossed the road to the station, entered it, and spoke to the stationmaster. He said, "A friend of mine is leaving town this morning. A nice jolly fellow, chunky sort of, in glasses, a cattle buyer."

"What train is he leaving on?" asked the stationmaster.

"The 7:51," said Townsend.

"Then you've missed him. The 7:51 has already come and gone, and I saw your man board it."

"You're sure it was the same man? Where did he buy a ticket for?"

"For Stop 17," said the stationmaster. "That's a lonesome stop in the Buck Rock country."

"If he made arrangements for shipping some cattle from here," said Townsend, "would you have the records yourself?"

"No," said the stationmaster. "Nor not at the freight office. That's a special department, handled down at the chutes. You'd have to go out to the edge of town and make your inquiry at the little office there."

Townsend walked out to the edge of town and made his inquiry at the little slab-boarded by the chutes. Nobody named Goodhue had made any arrangements to ship any cattle anywhere.

Sheriff Purdy in his office greeted Townsend with a warm smile, and offered him a cup of coffee which he declined.

The sheriff said, "Me and the county prosecutor sometimes trades little favors. You're going to start off your day bright and early by delivering a witness subpoena."

Townsend nodded.

"We got a big bully in town knowed as Rufe," said the sheriff. "Last night he stopped a city drummer in the alley behind the livery, scared him half to death with that pocketknife Rufe carries, honed to a razor's edge by the way, made him stand up straight and cut off all the buttons on his coat, one by one, down the front and even the cuffs, for the benefit of a little crowd. One of the crowd was a washerwoman, Kate Leahy. You're to deliver the paper to Kate."

"Where does she live?"

"She lives in a shanty just across from the back of the stable, but right now she's out at her daughter's cabin on Turtle Egg Creek, midwifin' the girl who has jest been a year married. It'll be a twelve-mile trip for you, out and back, but we cain't have these stunts going on."

"Of course not," said Townsend.

"Look at it this way," said the sheriff. "What if Rufe should try it on some thirteen-year-old mountain boy, and the boy would just reach out and take the knife away, and cut Rufe's throat. It's things like that that gives a place a bad name."

"A man like this Rufe ought to be horsewhipped," said Townsend. "And what will it get him? Maybe a couple of weeks in jail."

"Not even that," said Sheriff Purdy. "The judge will leave him off on probation."

Townsend was speechless.

"What it will get him is good and scared," said Sheriff Purdy. "A good scare might make a new man out of him. A couple of weeks in jail, and who would feed his pet bobcat? He loves that bobcat like its mother used to."

XII

It was on the ride back from Turtle Egg Creek, after serving his paper to the Widow Leahy, that a possible answer occurred to Townsend about the problem of the stolen cows from Mr. Alf Teague's front pasture, plus the reason Mr. Goodhue, so anxious to buy cattle, left town without making any arrangements to ship any, and yet looking so happy about it all.

Sheriff Purdy was in his office, at his desk, sandpapering the rust off of an old pair of handcuffs, when Townsend came in. He looked up and said, "I've got something to show you."

He pushed back his chair, led Townsend out into the narrow hall, down the hall to the rear, and they came to a stop by a grimy circular window at the top of the backstairs landing. The sheriff rubbed off some of the grime with his fingertips, gestured, and Townsend looked through.

He saw, in order, a sloping back roof—tin, a littered yard, an alley and across the alley a public hitching lot, almost deserted at this midafternoon hour. In one corner a two-by-twelve plank had been braced between two trees as a bench, and three men, in positions of ease, sat on the bench. They were WB men, Bill Blatchford himself, and his two gun throwers, Rad Devlin and the one with the buttermilk eyes.

"In town for trouble," observed Townsend.

" 'Fraid so," said the sheriff.

"In town looking for anything Lazy M," said Townsend.

"In town looking for you," said the sheriff.

"Me?" exclaimed Townsend.

"That's right," said the sheriff. "I heard they were strolling up and down around the town. And had a little visit with them. Bill Blatchford said they'd come in for a little talk with you. I didn't like the way he said it. I told him you were a deputy now, and he said not to bother him with trifles."

"Did he say what was bothering *him?*" asked Townsend.

"No. In fact he was too mad to do much talking."

"Well, I'm an easy man to see," said Townsend, and started down the steep backstairs.

Sheriff Purdy called: "Don't exceed your authority. And remember ain't none of them, includin' Bill, bluffers."

Townsend went down the steep dusty stairs, out through a back door, across the yard, across the alley, into the hitching lot and up to the men.

Blatchford, raising his bleached eyebrows slightly, looking every inch the old-style cattleman he was, said, "Once a wolfer, now a deputy. I had a feeling the sheriff would mention us and you'd come. Just look at him, boys, he reached that oath in time. You don't dare touch him now. He's been sworn."

Townsend saw nothing but hate and derision in their faces.

He said calmly, "I do hereby unswear myself. In other words, I call you. I don't like big mouths."

Nobody moved. Blatchforth said, "Don't tempt me."

"May I ask what all this is about?" said Townsend.

"Let's look into this a little," said Bill Blatchford. "Just who are you? The story I've heard is that you were hired by Alf Teague's brother, and come over the ridge into our valleys trying to catch up with a fellow who turns out to be Red River, Lazy M's new foreman. And what is the first thing you do after you get in? Why, you go directly to Lazy M. Up to this point there doesn't seem to be much else than Teague and Lazy M in yore background."

"True," said Townsend.

"Then, after a bit," said Blatchford, "you come to WB. And look it over. And make acquaintance with my head man, Dave Prentiss. Even come out in the dead of night, to bait him along."

"I liked him," said Townsend.

Blatchford ignored this. He said, "Nobody but you and him can ever know just what, everything, you said to him that night. You was makin' out to be his friend, but was setting him up for a kill.

And he was killed. You were working on Lazy M pay."

Rad Devlin got into the conversation. He said, "Taking Lazy M money then, and taking Lazy M money still. To my gunsight, a deppity taking private outside pay ain't no deppity at all."

Townsend didn't answer. He wheeled sharply, and left them.

Shortly after, he made a poker-faced report to the sheriff. The sheriff listened, enthralled. He said, "You'll do. All things considered, by that I mean considering you, you done about right. But don't go around unswearin' yourself whenever the whim takes you no more. Cain't nobody do that but me. I don't like the way this thing is suddenly whipsawin' us."

"I got my own ideas on that," said Townsend. "But maybe this ain't the time to go into them."

"Now's as good a time as any," said the sheriff. "The sooner, the better. Let's hear 'em."

Townsend gave his chin a short decisive shake, no!

Looking at the sheriff steadfastedly, he said, "Could there by any chance, any chance at all, be a merger, or a union, or something like that, undercover, between Lazy M and WB?"

Jarred, the sheriff said, "And that Bill Blatchford and Teague are really partners in the two outfits, and maybe even friends?"

"That's what I'm asking you."

"Not a chance in the world. There's a hundred ways the information would come to me. Was that one of your ideas?"

"No," said Townsend. "But I just wanted to get it out of the way. And you're sure you're not mistaken?"

"Quit talking like that," said the sheriff petulantly. "I've got enough trouble. Would you care to tell me what you were getting at?"

"No," said Townsend.

After a moment, he said, "But I can tell you one thing. Mr. Blatchford and his two gunmen didn't bring all that iron into town just for me. I'm just milkweed down to them, being sucked into the dust-devil because they've decided to clean up the whole thing, here and now. If you think you've got trouble, I'd say your real trouble is just getting ready to explode."

"The possibility occurred to me," answered the sheriff placidly.

"Well," said Townsend. "Widow Leahy has her paper and is anxious to testify. What shall I do next?"

"You could go down to the Acme Poolroom, like my other deputies, and maybe go to sleep in a chair with a bottle of beer, or you could walk up and down Main Street and sort of keep an eye on things."

"On Main Street?" said Townsend. "Doesn't Martinsburg have a town marshal?"

"I've often wondered that myself," said the sheriff.

As Townsend headed for the door, the sheriff said, "And always remember one thing."

"What's that?"

"A soft answer—not a hand-forged bowie knife—turneth away wrath."

"Oh, I wouldn't forget that," said Townsend gravely. "No, sir. Not that!"

This was the quiet hour, before the little flurry of presupper business, and Main Street lay peaceful, almost dozing. The merchants hadn't even begun to take in the coats and harness and hams and other merchandise hanging for display over the boardwalk, or the crockery and cheap hardware and ladies' bonnets from the plank tables which lined their window fronts. The air was crisp enough by now to faintly show a man's breath, and drive habitual loafers just inside doorways.

About a block and a half down from the courthouse, the marquee over the walk came to an end for the last half block, and continued past the cross-street corner as Main continued. This last half block was vacant, with the stubble of scythed autumn weeds, and two privately owned scrap lumber henhouses at its rear. The last building in the row, as you came to it, was a saloon.

It was square, cheap-framed, two-storied, once a barn red, now drab and colorless. The lower story, Townsend knew, was saloon, the upper a Saturday night dancehall. Big letters said: *The Paradise.* It catered to visitors and out-of-towners who knew no better.

There was a hitchrack at the road's edge, then the walk, of beaten earth here for merchants put down their own boardwalks, then a short walk of brick, then the saloon's front door with the sign: *We Never Close.*

Two men came out of the door and stood blinking in the sunlight. They were the WB gunmen Townsend had met just a short time ago—Rad Devlin, bowlegged and hard looking, and his vicious milky-eyed companion. A shot cracked out and the pale-eyed gunman collapsed. Devlin scurried back inside and slammed the door behind him.

Townsend turned around.

Across the street was an alley mouth between two buildings. Red River, the new Lazy M foreman, stood in the alley mouth, a rifle half to his shoulder. He stood there, out of accurate quick-shot pistol range, about as long as a man could count ten rapidly, then turned back at an easy lope into the alley.

Two things about this Townsend didn't like: Why, if he had killed one, didn't he kill the other? And why the deliberate interval of displaying himself before he retreated?

At a brisk run, Townsend crossed the street,

not directly, but at a diagonal for the corner.

The building on the corner happened to be wedge shaped. Townsend rounded the corner. A few feet beyond was the other opening of the alley. He dashed into it, slowed to a cautious, watchful stalk. He expected an ambush, and found one.

He had gone perhaps a hundred feet when he saw three beer barrels stacked against one wall, and Red River behind them, peering around them, his rifle at the ready, waiting for him.

All ready, snug behind this nice little fortification, was Red River ready to open fire. This was intended to be wholesale slaughter.

In a deadly flat voice, Townsend said, "Just lay your rifle and six-gun on the ground."

Red River turned, pumping shells wildly. Townsend shot him in his ugly mouth.

He went forward, turned the body over with his foot, and, hardly pausing, continued down the alley toward where Red River had just showed himself.

Across the street, a sinister little scene confronted him.

In the weed stubble of the corner vacant lot, about a dozen yards from the barnlike side of the saloon, stood a small clump of men: Bill Blatchford and his tough-looking little Rad Devlin, and Lazy M's new imports, the two gunmen in Levi's and their leader in his shabby batwing chaps and two well-kept six-guns. The Lazy M men stood in a sort of loose triangle, so their end men actually flanked Blatchford and Devlin. All guns were holstered, but there was definitely a feeling of shambles in the air.

Townsend walked up and stopped. He stopped about twelve feet away, in a position so that he was slightly offside of the entire group. They saw him, all of them, but no one acknowledged his presence.

Alf Teague was nowhere in sight.

The man in chaps, continuing a conversation with Bill Blatchford, said, "So the next time you take one of our front pasture cows we're going to rope you up in the hide and drop you into your own well. Do you know a final warning when you hear one?"

This wasn't to be a warning, Townsend knew, this was just a wordy build up to an execution.

In spite of the three-to-two odds against him, against obvious professionals at that, Blatchford said, "What do you mean, *our* cows? You never owned a cow in yore life, and I doubt if you ever even worked one."

"You blackguardin' me?" said the gunman, groping, trying to get this started and over with.

"I don't want any traffic with you trash," said Blatchford. "Step back. Yo're blocking me. I'm heading for the saloon."

"Who are you calling trash?" said the man in

chaps, trying to cover his lightning draw with a mock-angry voice. Mock-angry, Townsend knew, because the gunman cared not at all for words; he was simply earning his assassination money.

Townsend blew off the top of his head. He made a nice shot of it, because he was shooting at a target, not a man, and there was no more compunction in his trigger-finger than there was in the steel trigger itself. Around him, now, thunderous guns were roaring.

Rad Devlin proved better than the man in Levi's he selected, and slammed him skittering back and down with a shot in the heart and one for good luck in the belly—better than this man, but worse than his pal who shot and killed him as his gun muzzle scarcely left the leather rim of its holster. Then, with the odds so altered against him, two to one, he broke and ran. Bill Blatchford, no professional, but a passable amateur at that, put a .45 through his thighbone and brought him down with a crash, arms flailing.

Sheriff Purdy materialized in their midst.

"Yo're late," said Blatchford sourly.

"That's how I stay healthy," said the sheriff. "Anybody care to tell me about it?"

"They had me and Rad cornered," said Blatchford. "Then Deppity Townsend come up and exercised the law."

"You'll likely find a man inside the Paradise," said Townsend. "That friend of Mr. Devlin's. Red

River, the new Lazy M foreman, got him from that alley yonder."

"Where's this Red River now?" asked the sheriff.

"In the alley, I think," said Townsend.

"If you think so, I think so, too," said the sheriff.

The Lazy M gunman in the stubble was moaning.

"I winged that one," said Blatchford, "from behind."

"And you didn't demise him," said the sheriff.

"I just broke his thighbone for him," said Blatchford. "I thought sometimes when we didn't have nothing else to do, he might be interestin' to listen to in a court of law."

"I wonder where Mr. Teague is?" said Townsend.

"In my office waiting for me to come back," said the sheriff. "He dropped in on me to make a little speech and say if they was a range war he wanted me to understand it was in spite of him, that he wasn't having nothing to do with it, strictly. I couldn't hear the last of it too clear because of the gunshots."

"Do you think we could talk to him?" asked Townsend. "You and me and Mr. Blatchford here?"

XIII

As they walked down Main Street, Townsend said, "Sheriff, will you do me a favor?"

"I doubt it. I doubt it greatly. What is it?" asked the sheriff.

"Introduce me to Mr. Teague by some other name than Townsend."

"But he knows who you are!"

"Just do it."

"What name?" asked the sheriff. "I don't like this."

"Any name," said Townsend. "Any name at all."

Bill Blatchford said, "How about Taylor Harrison Leffingwell? That was the name of one of my mother's cousins. I don't see how you can beat it."

"That will be fine," said Townsend.

They found Mr. Alf Teague in the sheriff's office, slumped in the sheriff's chair behind the sheriff's desk. The short man in the fine broadcloth didn't seem so energetic at the moment. In fact, he seemed dejected, and his perpetually red-rimmed eyelids seemed to sparkle under nervous strain. When they came up to him, he said, "What was the gunfire?" The sheriff told him.

He listened, apparently appalled. Finally, he said, "What were they fussing about, Bill? What brought them to it, to killing each other?"

"Don't call me Bill," said Blatchford. "And you brought 'em to it. You sent 'em out to kill me."

"Why would I do a terrible thing like that?" said Teague, turning to Townsend and the sheriff for confirmation.

"Because you were trying to kindle up a little range war," said the WB owner.

"Because," said Townsend, "he was trying to get the mind of the county *on* a range war."

"Which he shorely did," said the sheriff. "But why?"

"To sidetrack them," said Townsend. "To do what he's been doing all along, but to do it this time in a big way because things were getting tight for him. To keep folks' attention away from Spruce Pasture."

"Spruce Pasture, and his best cattle?" Blatchford said.

"Spruce Pasture, and somebody's best cattle," said Townsend.

"Talk sense," said Teague, but there was a tenseness in him now.

"So now," said Townsend, "I can tell you about who took those front pasture cattle you've been layin' on Mr. Blatchford."

"I'd dearly love to know," said Teague.

"No one," said Townsend. "I told you a while back that maybe it was your own hands. I've changed my mind. Things looked that way to me at the time, but I've changed my mind. They was no cattle stole at all out of that front pasture, just reported stole. To keep attention off that back pasture."

"What's so special about that back pasture?" asked Blatchford.

"It's a marketplace," said Townsend. "For stole cows from probably far away. They go in and come out a back way. I'm sure you could find the way, and plenty of sign."

"Sheriff Purdy," said Teague. "We don't have to listen to this, do we?"

Townsend said, "I want a good long look in Spruce Pasture. To study a few brands."

"You ain't the first to want to pry around back there," said Teague.

"Sheriff," said Townsend. "Tell the gentleman who I am."

"I know who you are," said Teague. "Mark Townsend, a tramp wolfer turned deputy."

"Tell him," said Townsend.

Sheriff Purdy, looking as though he were being whipped into it, said, "Leave me to interduce Mr. Taylor Harrison Leffingwell."

"Major, retired," added Townsend suddenly impelled to fancy it up even a little more.

"And who in hell is that supposed to be?" asked

Teague, calmly, but showing faint signs of being disturbed.

Townsend said, “Chief Stock Detective for the K & R Cattle Association.”

Teague started to fall apart, then rallied.

“So what?” he blustered.

“I have three papers in my wallet,” said Townsend. “Authority from the Governor, identification from the Association, and a list of brands of stolen cattle. We’ve wondered about you for a long time. I’ve been sent here to do a little checking.”

There was a moment of utter, heavy silence.

“I don’t know how I got into it in the first place,” whispered Teague, wilting completely. “It started little and went big on me.”

“Lock him up, Sheriff,” said Townsend. “And get into Spruce Pasture as quick as you can.”

One night two weeks later, Holgate, the sheriff, and Townsend sat at Holgate’s kitchen table. Before each of them was a mug of Holgate’s lampblack coffee and in the center of the table was a quart bottle of white mule whisky.

Holgate picked up the bottle and poured a little whisky in the sheriff’s mug. “Say when,” he said.

“Suit yourself,” said the sheriff.

“Myself, I like sufficient,” said Holgate. “But I always stop before it changes the color of the coffee to look like spring water.”

“Why don’t you just pour the coffee in the whisky?” said Townsend. “You could control your proportions better.”

“Anybody like a dash of molasses to make it drinkable?” asked Holgate.

“Not me,” said the sheriff.

“Not me, either,” said Townsend.

“Nor do I,” said Holgate. “I like a whisky that’s always ready for a good fight. I don’t drink much or often, but when I do, I want the bugle to blow and the cavalry to charge.”

Each of them took a small, experimental sip.

“The telegraph is a wonderful thing,” said Sheriff Purdy, blinking rapidly. “They was stole cows in Spruce Pasture from as far away as Paris, France, almost.”

“Where is he now?” asked Holgate.

“Behind the safety of bars, and mighty glad to be there,” said the sheriff. “We got him dead to rights, and he’s talked faster’n a medicine man at the tailgate of his show wagon. He’s throwed hisself upon the mercy of the court.”

“On the mercy of a cow-country court?” said Holgate. “He must be scared crazy.”

“What about Mr. Goodhue, the buyer from the Buck Rock country?” asked Townsend.

“He talked, too,” said the sheriff. “They was stole Circle X cows in his possession. The man you seen by his campfire on the mountainside at Spruce Pasture with the Circle X horse had just finished negotiating some stole Circle X cattle with Teague. Mr. Goodhue went out to Lazy M, looked 'em over, and bought 'em. They went out the back way, o' course, the way they'd been brought in."

"Now I'll explain to you what you've been through," said the sheriff to Townsend, his true friendship for him, gleaming in his face.

"I know what I've been through," said Townsend.

"Only part of it," said the sheriff. "Lazy M hands was in on it, like you've been sayin', not all of 'em, just some of 'em, and they didn't do no rustling, just helped with the operation. So they had to be the right kind of men, just any waddy wouldn't do, too many are honest. The stuff was just brought in, and there disposed of by Mr. Alf Teague."

"And this Red River was a man he could use," said Holgate.

"Yes," said the sheriff. "He heard of him in a roundabout way and contacted him down in Colorado."

"And Red River got drunk down there," said Holgate. "And talked too much in Joe Teague's presence and Joe Teague followed him north here to Idaho. But why?"

"But why would you think?" asked Sheriff Purdy. "To force himself into such a payin' situation."

"And he wasn't wanted," said Townsend.

"Would you want him?" said the sheriff.

"No."

"He wasn't wanted," said the sheriff. "So he was stopped at Redstone Creek by two Lazy M men sent down for the purpose, Bobbie Ashburton and Ed Cushing."

"And this John Wilson," said Townsend, "the one who tried to kill me?"

"He was there at Redstone Creek, I'd guess," said the sheriff. "Even though you didn't see him. He was likely out of sight somewhere, covering his two pals, while they did what they'd been sent to do. Then he dropped back from the others when they left, to be sure you didn't follow them, which you did."

"Some humans I'll never learn to understand," said Holgate thoughtfully. "Alf Teague settin' them on him, layin' out orders to 'em to kill his brother."

Sheriff Purdy said, "When he tried to crawl into Alf's pocketbook he wasn't his brother anymore. He was just an enemy."

He drank down a third of his strange coffee. "I need a bracer for this. Now we come to the disagreeable part. It seems they was a scattering of rewards, mixed up and various and sundry, for certain cattle and certain men, herein involved. Added all up together, odds and ends, they come to quite a wholesome aggregate. I am obligated, no matter how you look at it, Mark, to fork over half to you, blast it!"

"How nauseatin'," said Holgate.

"But if I know Mark Townsend, he's going to act like a gentleman and refuse," said the sheriff hopefully.

"I'm going to take it," said Townsend.

"For what?" said the sheriff persuasively. "You're not one of these-here spendthrifts. Yo're sensible. Yo're contented jest to breathe in God's pure air, and eat stuff like wild weeds and lizards and half-cooked rabbits."

"Maybe he's going to leave my hearth and home," said Holgate, "and go out somewhere in a cedar thicket and buy himself a tepee."

"Apaches don't live in tepees," said Townsend. "They live in wickiups. And I'm not going to leave you and this house until you put me out. I'm going to take the money and buy into Bill Blatchford's WB, if he'll let me. Not to be a partner or anything like that, but just as an investment. I mean I'll promise not to mess around with the way he runs it. That'll be entirely up to him. If he'll let me do it."

"He'll do it," said Holgate.

Sheriff Purdy said, "From the mood he's in with you at the moment, he give it to you."

Minutes went by. They rehashed the thing over and over. The bottle of crystal-clear white mule got lower and lower. The big tin clock on the shelf above the range read: 11:02. Sheriff Purdy, shifting abruptly on his chair, said, "Well, you've got to go."

"Don't leave us now, Sheriff," said Holgate. "We're jest settlin' down."

"Not me," said the sheriff, pointing to Townsend. "Him. I'm not going anywhere."

"And where am I going?" asked Townsend.

"They's a westbound train coming through in about a half hour," said the sheriff. "The sizable towns along the way have been notified. Two men whose terms has expired at the Montana State Penitentiary will be on it. Both of them is blue-eyed, and both on the short side. One has gray hair, and the other is balder'n a goose egg. You can tell them because they'll be together and because of their prison shoes. What they've done in the past, what is knowed, couldn't be wrote and published in any newspaper. And though they're both past sixty, they're just getting started."

"What am I supposed to do?" asked Townsend.

"To remember what I told you. That a soft answer turneth away wrath. Jest politely tell them not to get off, that Martinsburg ain't in no need of them, for them to keep right on moving."

Townsend nodded.

"Naturally," added the sheriff, "if an emergency should come up, and you should raise their tempers a little, you'd have to handle it. You cain't send for the law. You *are* the law. And it would be nice for them always to remember it later."

"I understand that, too," said Townsend.

"You know what?" said the sheriff. "Some morning yo're going to wake up, and look in Mr. Holgate's mirror yonder, and see a medium-good lawman."

Center Point Large Print
600 Brooks Road / PO Box 1
Thorndike, ME 04986-0001 USA

(207) 568-3717

US & Canada:
1 800 929-9108
www.centerpointlargeprint.com